HUMBLE PARTINGS

THE THIRD HUMBLE GREETINGS NOVEL

ESSIE POWERS

BLOCKED

With the morning light creeping in through the window, Cassandra Harper felt the soft paper beneath her balled-up fist. Outside, she could hear the sound of summer rain drumming against the windowpanes. When she breathed in, she felt a strangely homey sense of warmth. There was something about Molinaar's Cottage — the headquarters of Humble Greetings — which made her feel more comfortable than she had ever previously felt. It was as if she had been blindly searching her entire life for a place to call her own and now she had found one. She had always believed that she was a Big City Girl, and she supposed some part of her still bought into that idea.

But she was here now.

This was her place for the time being.

She held the thick-leaded pencil lightly — it was so natural a position that she had long forgotten that once a teacher had trained her to do so. What she had achieved, she supposed, was nothing less than what any artist hoped to achieve. The pencil was now no more than an extension of her mind — her *imagination*.

Eyeing the page before her, she outlined the beautiful spring day inspired by a walk she had taken one afternoon with Robert's Jack Russell terrier, Woss. As always, she had taken her camera with her, snapping pictures of anything which drew her attention. She loved the way the simple act of taking the camera along had a habit of giving her a fresh impression. She might have walked a path a hundred times before but when she took her camera with her she never failed to see it as if for the first time.

Some previously unnoticed detail leaping through the lens.

She glanced to her current sketch, and then to the photograph she was using for inspiration. There was something off — no doubt about it. Some niggling detail she just couldn't place her finger on. She stared at the picture again. She looked for the usual suspects . . . things she usually had issues with. She looked to the tufts of grass, but they looked as well turned out as she managed them, sprouting from the muddy bank. Then she examined the sparkle off the water — light had always been one of her greatest frustrations, and yet it was so satisfying when she finally got it right.

But the light was fine.

One of her better efforts, even.

Finally, she addressed the sky. She had deliberately left it with minimal detail, not wanting to call too much attention to the back-drop . . . that sounded like something she had learned from someone in the past . . .

No, it was no good. Something was off about the composition.

With a frustrated sigh which cut through the otherwise mystical morning, she scrunched the paper into a ball and tossed it into the waste basket. Already filled to the rim with discarded paper, the ball bounced back out again.

She got up from where she had been hunched over her writing desk. She supposed she needed a cup of tea — that she needed a break from what she was doing . . . that was often the best method for loosening her creative blocks.

Was that what this was?

She trod barefooted over the cool kitchen tiles, passing Woss drowsing on his bed in the corner. She stuck the kettle on and turned her attention to the garden outside — to the dew draped over the grass like gossamer.

She took in her reflection in the glass. Her eyes looked larger than normal, and her strawberry-blond hair seemed wispier than usual — less substantial. Everything about her gaze was gaunt. Somewhat hollow. She thought about the cast-off comments from others she had accumulated over the past few weeks. Although she knew they hadn't been intended as personal affronts, she couldn't help but see them that way. All of those times when people had said she looked 'skinny' — not svelte, or 'in good shape' — and when on more than one occasion people had said she looked 'pale' or 'tired'. She supposed the truth of the matter was that things had changed; there was more work than she could ever have possibly imagined. But, then again, Humble Greetings wasn't just herself and Bella any more. Now it was a full-on enterprise. And thanks to Kareema Ashburton's Midas Touch — helped along by her assistant-cum-successor Sylvie — there was far more work than Humble could ever require.

Their future was assured.

And so why was her work coming so slow?

She poured the tea. This should've been the time she had waited for above all else — when there was no longer any sort of financial pressure upon her art. They had more orders than they could ever possibly hope for. Was it as simple as the increased demand? An upping of the stakes? Others depended on her now. Did her work come with more difficulty because she knew she had to keep on producing — that she had to constantly continue creating so they would always have something new to sell?

Logically, that seemed to be the nib of it . . . but what was she supposed to say?

Should she ask to reduce her workload?

Should she go to Robert and confront him about his business plans and arrangements, tell him she could no longer keep up with his demanding — some would say *punishing* — schedule? Then again, she knew just as well that if it hadn't been for meeting Bella, and the lingering discomfort at the prospect of somehow disappointing her, Cassandra most likely wouldn't have ever been making a living from her artwork.

How was it that she *wasn't* living her dream right now?

She mooched about the kitchen a while longer, trying to leaf her way through a magazine, but failing to get past the first few glossy pages of advertisements. Having finished her tea, she crouched down over Woss and gave him a gentle prod in the ribs.

He slept on, unperturbed.

No prospect of having an excuse to go out for a walk, then.

With her mind set on returning to work — on 'pushing herself through the process' — she headed back for the studio space. She hadn't made it more than a few steps down the hall, however, when she heard footfall on the stairs.

She looked up to see Bella.

As always, Bella was carrying a spiral-bound notebook, her ballpoint pen dangling out of the corner of her mouth. Upon seeing Cassandra, she pulled her pen free of her mouth, and grinned. "Wandering the halls for inspiration, too?"

Cassandra smiled. "Something like that."

Bella propped her elbow on the banister. "Whenever I want to jog my mind, I make myself a cup of tea."

"Done that."

"Really?" Bella sniffed the air. "Thought something smelled good — maybe that was what got me to my feet. Something subconscious, I guess." She sighed. "Well, that settles it. If tea can't get your creative juices flowing then what hope have you got?"

Feeling an inexplicably warm feeling rising in her throat, Cassandra felt a sudden urge to change the subject. She wasn't usually like this . . . so . . . *emotional.* "Where's Robert?"

"Oh, he's out."

"Where?"

Bella twiddled her fingers in the air, as if it was an unknowable truth. "With George and Harriet — something *business-related,* no doubt."

"A meeting?"

Bella shrugged. "Maybe."

Even though Cassandra knew Bella well enough from having lived with her for over a year, she was still rendered surprised by her nonchalant attitude to the administration of the business. When Robert — and then George and Harriet — had arrived, it was almost as if Bella had ceased to care about that aspect any longer. The change was especially marked since Bella had a solid business woman's head upon her shoulders from years working in the city. It was strange to think Cassandra had started out with little to no appreciation of business. She had always believed it to be the least important part of her plans. But — as she had realised over the time she had worked with Bella — it was the key to everything.

It was the key to artistic freedom.

That artistic freedom she possessed now.

"Look, Cass, I've been thinking — why don't you take some days off? Have a bit of a break?"

Cassandra felt her heart sink. "I . . . I should be okay."

Bella smiled and shook her head. "No, really — I'm insisting. Take a few days off. Come back refreshed. I'm going to take some time, too, but I'm planning to stay around here. Around the village."

Cassandra knew this euphemism well. Whenever Bella spoke in these terms, she meant she was going to go and visit her mother. Cassandra couldn't help but speculate as to whether Bella and Robert might be fighting. But — since she lived in close proximity to them, and had heard not the slightest hint of argument — she didn't believe this to be a likely explanation. Then again, perhaps they had other reasons for wanting Cassandra out of the house . . .

Cassandra drew a deep breath. Then she forced on a smile. "Okay," she replied. "Just a few days."

"Great — I'll help you pack."

2

A FEW DAYS OFF

assandra felt the breeze blowing back her hair as she stood on the drizzly, windswept platform of Unthorpe Train Station. The disposable cup of hot chocolate she held in her hands warmed her blood, keeping her alert. She looked up at the live departures screen in the fading daylight, as if the train's estimated time of arrival might magically shuffle closer. It had been tricky to select a place to go on holiday when she lived in Normonswold; when she did what she loved all the day through — it was as if every day was a holiday . . . and perhaps that was where the problem came in. How was she supposed to take a break from *that* . . .

Even despite Bella's best efforts, Cassandra had managed to sneak in a couple of sketchpads and more than enough pencils and pens to get her through the next days. Cassandra couldn't imagine not sketching during her time off, in the same way that she couldn't imagine doing without air for too long. Bella had made her promise, however, that she would not do any work for Humble

Greetings; that any drawings Cassandra created were wholly for her own purposes. In fact, Bella had gone so far as to claim that she wouldn't *accept* any work Cassandra did during her time off.

Cassandra glanced back up at the train departures, and was surprised to see the screen had now transformed. And that beside her own train was the explanatory note:

Cancelled.

She stared at the screen for the longest time, trying to divine more meaning from the phrase. But it was what it was:

Cancelled.

Feeling light-headed, she turned away from the platform, treading into the station building. There was nobody manning the station. The lady who had been selling tickets had left just after she had sold Cassandra her ticket — a little after five o'clock.

There was nobody to ask.

She drew in a deep breath, then walked her way out of the station building, back onto the road outside. There was nobody around. Only the houses of Unthorpe which began a little way away. She wondered what she was going to do. Bella had driven her here and dropped her off. There was of course no alternative for her but to call Bella back, and get her to pick her up again. If there was no train, then Cassandra wasn't going anywhere tonight.

As Cassandra dug through her bag for her phone, she noticed a car approaching — winding out of the roads of Unthorpe, not so far away. It was a hatchback, the wipers swishing back and forth. She tilted her head to one side, not quite able to comprehend the sight. Then some recognition sparked inside her mind.

It was Kieran Eric Doores . . . otherwise known as Dorothy.

As he drew closer in his car, she made out his facial features in more detail. How the tips of his long flaxen hair brushed his shoulders. He pulled into one of the spaces. As he stepped out of the car,

Cassandra saw he was wearing a suit; that he had clearly just come from work. When he looked up and recognised her, he froze misstep. Slowly, a smile formed on his lips. Then his arms opened wide. "Cass!"

Cassandra had no time to hide as he threw his arms about her, crunching her into a hug. When she had finally peeled herself away from Dorothy's embrace — hopefully with all of her ribs intact — she mentioned her dilemma. "The trains are all cancelled."

" 'Cancelled' ?" Dorothy replied, furrowing his brow. His puppylike enthusiasm was broken for the first time. He seemed to reel himself back just as quickly, an uneasy smile returning. "Why are they cancelled?"

"I don't know — there was no other information."

Dorothy blinked to himself for several moments, as if trying to clear a daze in front of his eyes. Then he looked back to Cass. "Where're you trying to get to?"

"Pawler's Bay."

"The coast?"

Cassandra nodded.

"Okay, all right. I can drive you if you like?"

Cassandra felt herself bowled back. "Oh, really, that's fine. It's a long way — an hour's drive . . . more, maybe?"

Dorothy, however, waved his hand at her, as if physically scattering her concerns from the air. "No, no. It's no problem at all." He dug through his inside jacket pocket, producing his phone. "Just let me make a call, all right?"

Cassandra had no idea what to say. But she was hardly going to turn down Dorothy's generosity. And it wasn't like she would be able to get anywhere under her own steam tonight. She watched on as Dorothy disappeared around the corner, his phone to his ear, a deep look of concern sketched across his features.

She wondered who he might be calling.

When Dorothy returned, any sense of his dark mood was gone. Perhaps the phone call had acted as some sort of reassurance. Cassandra, too, had had a chance to think about the offer on the table. "Look, if you could get me as far as Erma's Brook that would be fine. I could catch a bus from there."

Dorothy shook his head vigorously. "No, no. I'll take you there. It's not too far out of my way."

Cassandra knew this to be a lie, considering Dorothy *lived* in Unthorpe . . . where they were right now. Then again, she didn't know for sure that Dorothy planned to go straight home . . .

She thought through her options. It would be exceedingly odd for her to return to Molinaar's Cottage when Bella had made such a song and dance about her going away for a few days. She looked at Dorothy. "If you're sure you wouldn't mind?"

Dorothy held up his hands. "I'm sure I wouldn't mind."

"Okay, then."

The two of them got into Dorothy's car.

Cassandra felt overwhelmed, as she always did whenever she sat in Dorothy's car. She took stock of the car seats — covered in that fuzzy, deep-purple material. There was an artificial scent of peaches and cream inside too, although this was overwhelmed by the smell of coffee; the source of which she soon realised was the pile of empty cups piled up in the back seat floor space. A teddy-bear shaped car freshener hung from the rear-view mirror. The teddy bear looked as though it had seen better days.

Once they were on the open road, Cassandra couldn't help but feel a sense of freedom skip through her heart. Her entire body felt lighter. She felt as if she was stepping out on a grand new adventure. Even though they had made the trip up to Scotland — the past year — so that they might visit Kareema Ashburton in her home, that hadn't been in any way relaxing. That had been work-related. Everything she did nowadays was worked-related.

And yet, she *loved* her work . . .

Dorothy just drove, hardly uttering a word to her once they had left Unthorpe behind, and they were well on their way. She could only guess at what he might be thinking. Although he had been a constant presence in her life during the year or so she had been living in Normonswold, she could hardly say she knew him any better than when she had arrived. The only aspect which stood out to her was that he had a penchant for wearing women's clothing. So, with this in mind, and realising that they were probably only fifteen, twenty minutes from their destination, she turned to him. "Do you ever feel as if something's missing in your life?"

Dorothy gripped the steering wheel, continuing to guide them along the winding, looping, ups and downs of the back-country lanes. "In what way 'missing' ?"

"You know . . ."

"You mean *someone* missing — you mean *loneliness?*"

Cassandra was somewhat disarmed by Dorothy's no-nonsense tone. How he cut right to the nub of what she was saying. She almost wanted to walk things back — to deny this was what she had meant at all.

"Yes, I suppose," Cassandra replied.

A smile caught the corner of Dorothy's mouth. "It must feel like you're in some real-life domino stunt."

"What'd you mean?"

"You know, stand up all the dominos in a row, knock one down . . . the *Domino Effect.* You know what I mean." Dorothy smiled wider then slipped Cassandra a sidelong glance. "First Bella, then Harriet . . . you can't tell me you haven't noticed you're the last maiden at Humble Greetings."

Cass's ribcage squeezed her lungs. She felt it difficult to form a response. Then she looked out of the window at the passing grassy banks, and the sunlight fading over the fields. The golden sunrays giving the whole terrain one last breath of life.

"It's not jealousy," she said, unable to believe she was even having this conversation.

"I know."

"It's just . . . something." She turned back to Dorothy. "It might not even be *someone* — maybe it is just the amount of work. The *pressure* on me to produce more and more. To create better artwork. Not to be the reason that Humble fails."

Dorothy said nothing. Then — out of nowhere — he dragged the car hard to the left.

Cass's heart leaped into her mouth. She smashed into the car door. She grabbed the sides of her seat, trying to remain stable, not wanting to be caught off balance by the recoil as the car straightened out its trajectory.

They were headed up a dirt track now, the tyres crunching over the loose rocks.

Pleasantly muddy fields on either side.

"Sorry about that," Dorothy said, "almost missed the turning."

A hint of distrust entered her mind. She didn't know Dorothy at all. Just because Bella and everyone else in and around Normonswold trusted him didn't — by extension — mean she should too. "Is this the quickest way?" Cassandra finally got out, impressed that she managed to make her voice sound so confident; so unshaken.

"No. Actually, we're going out of our way, but trust me, it'll be worth it, okay? We're almost at Pawler's Bay. Just ten minutes up the road when we go back on ourselves."

Cassandra turned her attention front and centre. She took stock of the dirt track ahead. And tried to keep an open mind. She really couldn't believe the course this evening had taken. If her train had arrived on time, then she would've been getting into Pawler's Bay Station around now. And she wouldn't have run into Dorothy at all.

At the end of the fields there was a grove, and the dirt track soon turned back to asphalt. The ride smoothed over, and Cassandra shifted her attention onto the scene opening up ahead. The sea.

As the sun dipped below the horizon, it set the surface of the water aflame.

The waves were beautifully smooth, tranquil, as they lapped into the pebble beach nestled in the cove below. She could make out the jaggedly arranged cottages, all of them painted cheerful seaside tones of blue, pink, yellow. She felt she was a million miles from the more sombre surroundings of Normonswold right now.

Dorothy parked up and they got out.

All at once, Cassandra felt the damp sea breeze against her cheeks. She tasted the salt settling at the back of her throat, and felt a gentle throb humming through her veins. She could hear the sweep of the tide on the pebble beach. It drew the water back, and then released it, allowing it to flow in-land.

She thought about a sketch she had once done when she had been younger, and had had somewhat more surrealist tastes. She had drawn a giant mermaid at the bottom of the sea, lying on his back, breathing the tides into his chest before exhaling them. As she stood on this cliff, overlooking the bay, she could almost believe that the sound of the water rushing in over the beach was like that giant's respiration.

Perhaps there had been some truth to that particular adolescent madness.

"Ready?" Dorothy finally asked, when they had been there for a good five, ten minutes.

Realising she was smiling, Cassandra nodded.

3

THE BAY

*C*assandra stood on the street corner of the hotel she had booked for her days off. She watched as Dorothy departed, trundling up the street and away. Once he had turned the corner, she felt a sudden sense of loneliness grip her. It was almost overpowering.

And yet she had felt this way before.

In some ways, she supposed she had been spoiled. Ever since she had got involved with Humble Greetings, she had had people around her all the time. There had never been a chance for her to feel lonely because there wasn't so much as a moment to think.

She turned on the spot, unable to get over the sight of the sea ahead. There was something so grand, so overwhelming about the sea. Something which reminded her of just how insignificant she really was. About the all-consuming power of nature. If she strode into those waves she would be crushed.

Pulled beneath them.

Thrown about like a ragdoll, and then drowned.

She couldn't help wondering if those that lived by the sea didn't do so as a means of testing their resolve. As a means of seeing just how strong they really were. Just how firm they could stand against the forces of the world.

With night closing in, Cassandra knew there wasn't much time, so she checked into the hotel, leaving her bags up in the guest room. She made for the beach with her sketchbook and drawing materials, determined to take advantage of the sunset. She sat herself on the smooth pebbles and brought her sketchbook onto her lap. There seemed nothing more natural in the entire world than to feel the tip of her pencil against the paper. To be caressing the page.

No conscious thought went into what she drew. And once she had completed one page, she moved onto the next. And then the next. When she eventually surfaced — hearing a group of voices drifting over the beach — she had to flip back through the pages to remind herself of just what she had drawn. Already, she could see the different shapes. Things which would never have occurred to her back in Normonswold. Perhaps there had been more logic than she had truly appreciated in getting away from the village for a few days. It would replenish her pool of inspiration.

And she was just getting started.

She set her sketchpad down at her side, on the pebbles, and glanced over at the approaching people. There were six or seven of them. A pair carried cameras, while another bore a microphone at the end of a pole — from friends she had spoken to who had become involved in show business, she recalled the person being called a 'boom man', or something similar. Another trio walked along with headphones hanging about their necks. All of them had a clipboard. Cassandra was brought into mind of cattle due to the cacophony they made treading their way along the beach. She decided it was time to take a night-time walk along the promenade before seeing where she might be able to get some dinner.

The next morning, Cassandra woke to the smell of cooked breakfast wafting beneath her bedroom door. She could hardly believe her luck when she recalled her stay included a Full English Breakfast, replete with eggs, beans, sausages, bacon, fried mushrooms and tomatoes, hash browns, buttered toast, and a cup of black coffee.

Back at Molinaar's Cottage she was in the habit of working late into the night and waking a little before noon the next day. Last night, however, she had gone to bed early. Perhaps there was something about being in a different place which affected her.

Which made her long to go out and explore.

Once she had chomped her way through breakfast, she set out for a walk along the beach. The sun was shining down once again, and the glittering tide was washing over the pebbles. There was an older lady with a grizzled black Labrador trotting through the foam which had been thrown up by the sea.

Cassandra sat down and brought out her sketchpad, beginning to draw the scene. It was nothing more than a rough sketch — again just an extension of her mind. When the woman approached, she felt a twinge of apprehension. As the woman strode past, the dog lagging at her heels, Cassandra exchanged a dampened "Morning" and turned the page of her sketchbook so the woman wouldn't see what she had drawn.

Throughout the rest of the morning on the beach, Cassandra saw nothing else. As she sat propped against the rocks, the sun gained in strength. She felt its rays beating down upon her shoulders, warming her face, neck and exposed forearms. She was wearing jeans and hadn't packed anything for warm weather. She hadn't even had the foresight to bring a bathing suit. As lunchtime approached, she decided to amend this last detail, trudging over the village promenade, and peering in through shop windows until she had come across what she sought.

It was a shop full of everything for the beach.

She dug about the inventory until she uncovered a serviceable beach towel and a swimsuit which wouldn't have been seen on any catwalk this century but would serve a purpose here. There was nobody she *knew* who would judge her dress sense.

After returning to her hotel to put the swimsuit on underneath her clothes, she found herself a spot of lunch at a café with a terrace overlooking the beach. She ordered a bowl of tomato and basil soup, deciding against the fish specials. She had never really been much of a fan of fish.

When the proprietor emerged from the café and offered to put up the parasol to guard her from the sun's glare, Cassandra waved her away with a smile. It seemed unnatural for her to deny the sun when it was making her feel so warm and wonderful.

Finished with lunch — ordering a cool glass of freshly squeezed lemonade by way of a dessert — she made her way back down to the beach.

The day had really opened out before her now. The sea stretched off to the horizon, and the surface of the water was an immaculately smooth mirror. She took stock of the ships in the middle distance — almost lost to the haze — as they trundled through the calm waters. She drew what was before her eyes, hardly even looking down at the page as she did so. She felt herself entering a trancelike state, her whole body relaxing into her work.

Into what she had been placed on this earth to do.

Humble had never been as far away from her as it was now. It was only when she came up for air, when she took swigs from the bottle of water she had brought down to the beach with her, that she even remotely turned her thoughts to her day job . . . to all of the greetings cards which still needed to be designed.

It was late-afternoon — and the sun was dipping down into the horizon — when she surfaced from her page. Her heart was beating so low. And her pulse was so steady.

She stripped off her outer layer of clothing and went down to the sea wearing her newly acquired swimsuit, clutching her beach towel close to her chest, as if it might protect her from some unseen enemy. She waded into the waves and bobbed about in the water, inhaling deeply, feeling her whole body stretching out and becoming a part of the sea. When she had had enough of swimming, she returned up the beach, hardly needing to dry herself in the strong sunlight. With her towel hanging over her shoulders, she flipped through the sketchbook, surprising herself to see just how much work she had completed.

She had barely a single conscious recollection of what she had done.

She had simply slipped away to another place.

All of those sights and sounds, emotions and sensations, which'd passed through her as she had drawn. They all flickered back into her mind. It was like flipping through a reel of her memories in concrete form. So much more complete than a photograph.

She had captured moments.

As Cassandra rose up, readying herself to go and find some dinner in the village, she noticed the group from the night before. That film crew, or whatever they were. They were huddled into a half circle, speaking amongst themselves as if they were some sort of top-secret organisation. Cassandra felt a spike of anger in her gut. It was unlike her to have such a vociferous reaction to someone or something.

But it felt like an intrusion.

As if Pawler's Bay should belong to her and her alone.

As if she had some kind of an unshakeable claim to this place.

And yet the voice of reason cut through her thoughts, reminding her that this was a public location. And that the village belonged to all.

As she headed back up the beach, to the refuge of the village, she couldn't help but feel outraged that soon the images the film crew were capturing would be shared with the world. What had seemed so personal — so *private* — would belong to anybody who saw the footage.

Try as she might, Cassandra couldn't find sleep that night. She supposed it might have something to do with the humidity. Or the fact that she was going to bed much earlier than she normally would. Tonight, she wasn't as worn out as she had been the first night. On the contrary, she felt energised . . . ready to do just about anything.

After she had been tossing and turning for what seemed like hours, she finally gave up. She slipped back into her jeans and put a blouse on over her pyjama top. There was nobody on reception at the hotel at this time but the door — as with any of the doors in this town — was unlocked. She stepped out into the sea air, once again feeling as if she was being bathed in previously unknown elixir.

She ventured through the dimly lit village, back down to the beach, expecting it to be deserted. For it to only be illuminated with moonlight. For the stars to fill the never-ending sky above like sprinkled glitter. She was already halfway before she realised she had forgotten her sketchpad and was toying with the idea of returning, when she saw that the beach wasn't as vacant as she had expected.

The film crew were there.

All half dozen of them.

The pair of cameras shone bright, false lights all over the pebble beach. There was something alien about the landscape — about these *invaders* . . .

Feeling a sense of disgust overcoming her, Cassandra turned away from the film crew, deciding that she might as well return to her hotel room and draw from memory.

However — just as she prepared to turn back — someone called out.

"Hey!"

She took a step back to the village.

"Hey!"

She paused, glanced around.

And immediately scolded herself for doing so.

She should've just kept on walking — should've not acknowledged the call.

But now it was too late.

She stood still, seeing the person who had called out was approaching, jogging towards her. It was one of the men who had been holding a clipboard.

As he closed on her, she couldn't help but notice the firm, square shape of his jaw. How his hair was a medium, slightly unkempt; strong and bristling — a deep, black tone. As he approached, he dropped his arms to his sides, and Cassandra couldn't help but notice that he looked as if he had the type of body which was acquired from an adventurous lifestyle rather than a few hours in a gym.

"Hi," he said, smiling wide, and a touch nervously, Cassandra thought.

"Hello."

"I've, uh, seen you around . . . on the beach . . ." he nodded to her then gestured with his hand ". . . usually you've got something . . ."

"A sketchpad?"

He grinned wider, meeting her gaze. She realised his eyes were perfect almond shapes. "Yeah, that's right . . . a sketchpad. You're an artist, I guess?"

Cassandra felt her throat constrict. Even though she knew the man's assertion was nothing but the truth, she still felt the weight of the word. It was something she had striven to be for so long and yet she felt squeamish about owning it.

Why?

"Yes," she replied, and then, because it felt like the right thing to say. "I design greetings cards — Humble Greetings?"

The man gave her a blank expression, but, then again, when would she ever expect a man to recognise something so ephemeral as the brand of cards he bought or received? "Is that why you're here? Looking for more inspiration for greetings cards?"

Hearing one of the film crew calling out, Cassandra turned in that direction. They were trying to get this man's attention. "Um, kind of . . ." she replied.

"Well, if you wouldn't mind terribly, I was just wondering — *we* were just wondering — if you'd ever done any sort of story-boarding . . . you know, sketches for scenes to be filmed?"

"I . . . can't say I have . . . not really, anyway . . ."

The man batted his hand, as if to physically dismiss her concerns. "Nothing to it — only that I reckon it'd be awfully simple compared to what you're used to . . . in fact, I'm *certain* it'd be way beneath you."

Even though Cassandra knew he was smothering her with flattery, she couldn't say she was fully resisting his charms. What kind of a person could hand-on-heart say that they disliked being told they were exceptional?

And then there was the uncomfortable truth that she didn't want to leave this man's company just yet. In fact, she wanted to do whatever she held in her power to stay with him. Just out of curiosity, of course.

"What'd you need doing?"

The man smiled wider and took a step towards her. "It's nothing, really. We're filming the coast for a documentary, and, well, we just can't quite seem to get the sequence of shots right." He nodded to the film crew over his shoulder. "That's the director, over there, making a racket" — Cassandra could see the round figure of the director had taken a break from attempting to get this man's attention, instead busying himself with one of the cameramen — "and I'm the *assistant* director."

Cassandra met his eyes again, seeing warmth and kindness . . . or perhaps that was her own personal projection. Maybe she was just seeing what she *wanted* to see . . . she thought back to the conversation she had had with Dorothy on the way here, and thought about how he had spoken of the Domino Effect.

Was she longing to see something that wasn't really there?

Just so she could belong to the Couples' Club?

"We'd pay you, of course," the man went on. "You being a professional, and all."

"All right. What'd you need?"

He brought the clipboard up to the moonlight. She saw outlines of the boxes into which the sketched shots were supposed to be placed. "We already have a fair idea about what we want — it's really just a case of being able to *visualise* things." He glanced back over his shoulder to the rest of the film crew, then leaned in close, in a cartoonish conspiratorial manner. "Our director is very big on being able to *visualise* things." He then made the frame of a cinema screen with his thumbs and index fingers.

Cassandra couldn't help but smile.

"We just need a few shots of the coastline, an idea about how they will fit together, you know? With presenters travelling from one place to another there needs to be a sense of movement — an idea that they might've stopped off at the train station and taken a stroll along the beach before they appear on camera, something like that, okay?"

Cassandra felt a touch overwhelmed, but she managed a smile back. "Okay."

"So," the man said. "Can I leave this with you? See what you can come up with? You're not planning on leaving early tomorrow, are you?"

Cassandra shook her head. "No, I'm not leaving."

The man smiled back. "Good. I'm glad. My name's Finnegan— *Finn.*"

"I'm Cassandra. *Cass.*"

With that, he left Cassandra with the clipboard.

And a stomach full of butterflies.

4

RAINBOW DUST PRODUCTIONS

inn watched her turn the corner — as she disappeared into the night. His heart was beating rapidly. A cool sweat had broken out on his brow. Even as she left him behind, it was impossible to forget her.

Her delicate, dormouse features.

Her hair bouncing against her back in the warm night air.

He only returned to reality when he heard Peter Hauntspath — the director — calling out to him once again. As he ventured down the pebble beach, his feet slipped and slid with the loose stones. He stumbled several times, but managed to retain his balance. Despite the beauty of this particular spot, he would be glad to get back to the real world, with its firm ground underfoot, and its seven-eleven opening hours. He supposed he had always been a City Boy at heart. The Great Outdoors had never really been much of a factor in his upbringing. If his current project hadn't brought him here — to Pawler's Bay — he didn't suppose he ever would've come.

Upon returning to the others, he saw things were ticking along just as cluelessly as before. It seemed par for the course for Rainbow Dust Productions. What had he been thinking when he had taken on work from a company with such a name? What had he *expected* from a company with such a name? And yet, he had applied, and he had spoken to Peter, and Peter had been so flattering and so determined to have him on board . . . and the project had sounded — well, it had sounded just so . . . *standard.*

They were supporting the primary film crew which was working with a trio of presenters travelling the land, exploring the nooks and crannies of Great Britain, drinking in the countryside. Rainbow Dust Productions was tasked with getting some establishing shots. When Peter had pitched him the idea, he had made things sound so simple. For one, Finn had believed Peter had at least had all the locations in mind for where they would shoot footage . . . but this had soon proven to be a hopelessly optimistic assumption.

The cameramen were trudging their way along the pebble beach, grabbing tracking footage of nothing much more than stones and sand. Unable to keep himself from doing so, Finn looked to Peter, seeing whether or not he had a better idea about his vision. Peter was a man of about sixty, with shaggy silver hair, a thriving beard and a protruding gut. He had all sorts of stories about adventuring in faraway, foreign lands. There was one thing which was certain about Peter. His days of marauding adventure — if they had ever even existed at all — were behind him.

Peter was still standing with his feet shoulder-width apart, hand cupping his chin, examining the scene as if it was the most profound spectacle he had ever witnessed.

Finn felt a shudder pass across the surface of his skin. He hated to feel like this; to feel impotent to stop what was happening.

Perhaps he had been lucky, but he had never run across this issue previously. He had never found himself at the mercy of a clueless director.

Because it helped him keep his mind off the mediocrity of the project they were creating, Finn shifted his attention up the beach, back to where he had seen Cassandra disappearing among the seaside cottages. Even now, he couldn't help but congratulate himself — just a little — that he had achieved some masterstroke. Not only had he managed to get talking to a beautiful girl, he had also established she was an artist — although that had been somewhat obvious given her sketchpad, the infinite patience with which she had sat on the beach drawing. It had been an impulse to ask her to do them a storyboard, and one which might yet bear fruit. He turned back to Peter, and the cameramen, seeing they were still taking shots of pebbles.

If this outing wasn't to prove a complete waste of time then he had better wrestle control of the project himself . . . albeit with a subtle grace which gave Peter the Director no hint as to what was occurring.

And then there was the question of Cassandra.

He did hope he hadn't scared her off.

5

HOLLYWOOD CALLING

*A*s Cassandra strolled the promenade the next morning, she couldn't help but think she could easily get used to a Full English Breakfast each and every day. There was something about starting the day with such a hearty meal which filled her with strength. She didn't suppose such a diet was entirely recommended on health grounds, though, and decided when she returned to Normonswold she would probably be better off sticking with her standard diet of unbuttered toast, porridge and a glass of orange juice.

Today was just as flawless as the others had been. The blue sky soared off into the distance. Half a dozen ships bobbed on the water. Seabirds glided on gentle thermals, breaking the otherwise complete silence and stillness with their cackles.

Cassandra took up her spot on the beach. As she surveyed her surroundings, she couldn't help but feel a slight note of disappointment to realise the film crew wasn't there. Although on previous days, they had been nothing but an intrusion, she hadn't quite been able to get Finn off her mind. And he had set her an assignment — so there was an excuse for her to *want* to see him . . .

That said, when Cassandra had returned to the hotel, it hadn't been to get to work on the storyboard which Finn expected of her. It had to be the sea air which was to blame, as she had felt herself carried off to sleep before she had so much as been able to press her pencil lead to the page.

And now she would need to dedicate this morning to the storyboard.

As she propped herself against the rocks, she already had ideas in mind about what she was going to sketch for Finn. She had only been a little modest when she had claimed she had not really done any storyboarding. Back in the City, she had done a couple of storyboards for friends' art projects. On a couple of occasions she had done some work for advertisements, though she had found it difficult to stoke any passion once the entire composition was so firmly leaned towards a single purpose:

Selling.

She thought about what Finn had given her. To be quite honest, it really wasn't all that much of a brief. He wanted footage to suggest a quick stop on the way. That the presenters — whoever they were — in the duration of the programme — whatever that was — would stop in at Pawler's for a fleeting visit. And it was Finn and his filmmakers' task to capture the essence of the fake visit.

And it was her task to create some kind of a spark.

Just as she had done with her sketches for the past few days, Cassandra pressed her pencil to the page and began to outline what came to mind — what the scenery impressed upon her. It was as if all of her senses became heightened in the moment. As if she fell headlong into the world which surrounded her. The gentle

29

washing of the tide over the pebbles. The cackling gulls overhead. The rumbling boats in the distance.

By the time she surfaced, she realised her exposed face and neck had grown hot. When she glanced at her watch, she saw it was already past midday. She looked down at the work she had produced on the storyboard — quietly happy with her efforts. Whenever she drew just for herself, she was never quite sure whether or not what she was creating was any good at all. But when there was a firm focus ... when she was working for somebody else, there was hardly ever a doubt in her mind.

Cassandra retreated to a nearby café and ordered herself a cool glass of lemonade, while she retrieved a bottle of after-sun lotion she had bought the day before and stowed in her bag this morning — rather sagely, it seemed.

Still near to bursting from the Full English Breakfast, she made a point of asking the proprietor for the smallest sandwich on the menu. As she sat chewing on her lunch, she turned her focus onto the sketch she had produced that morning — onto the storyboard she had created for Finn.

She wondered if there had been a time when she had been so keen to impress others it had utterly overwhelmed all else. She supposed there must have been. Maybe back when she had been a teenager. Back when she had just started to sketch away ...

Now, though, she was convinced of her abilities. It was no longer like she was capturing some ether in a bottle and holding it up for inspection, as if they might be able to interpret what it was all about simply by turning their head to one side and squinting. Now Cassandra had learned all the tricks about how she could communicate to others through nothing more than the medium of her drawings. And she was convinced that the work she had done on the storyboard would communicate clearly enough to Finn.

She finished lunch. She balanced whether or not she would return to the hotel for a nap, before returning to the beach for an evening session with her sketchpad. There were a few clouds dotting the sky. Her face felt a little tingly from the sun. As she prepared to turn away from the scene, in favour of her bed, she noticed the film crew making their way along the promenade.

The director walked with his hands in his pockets, head down, leading what could only be interpreted as his fatigue-riddled team in his wake. She spotted Finn among them, in animated conversation with the man carrying the microphone. He noticed her without the need for her to so much as wave. She watched on as the smile pulled back the corners of his mouth and felt a warm sensation in the pit of her gut. He got the attention of the team, and they all — *albeit a mite reluctantly* — made for her direction.

"Evening," Finn said, leading the group, striding alongside the director.

Cassandra felt her heart bounce up to her throat. Her ribcage tightened. She felt for a horrible second as if she was sinking. But arrested her descent. "Hi," she replied, tearing her attention away from Finn's eyes, and back to the real world.

The director was a man in his mid-sixties with choppy, neck-length silver hair, a slight paunch and chubby, babylike cheeks. "Peter Mills," he said, affecting an elaborate bow, complete with a whole lot of elegant twirling of his hand. "And this is the crew."

She looked to the others. They all wore weary expressions, but made the effort to raise their voices in some form of greeting. She couldn't help but get the idea that they wanted to be anywhere else than here.

"So," Peter said, slipping Finn a glance, "Finn had the bright idea of asking you to do a little storyboarding for us."

She sensed a slightly abrasive tone to his words and couldn't help but wonder if there wasn't an element of friction between him and Finn.

She brought her sketchbook up. The director took it from her.

She stood silently by as his eyes skimmed back and forth, absorbing the contents of the panels. She couldn't help but hold her breath. It didn't matter she had mentally grasped the idea she was designing cards for millions of people, there was still a raw fear associated with standing before a live crowd and presenting her work.

The whole film crew crowded around — all of them interested.

She couldn't help but wonder if this wasn't a reflection on the director's leadership. That they were so desperate for ideas that they were willing to give any sort of outside inspiration a try.

The director — Peter — cupped his chin in his palm. "Well, I think this could work."

The cameramen exchanged a glance behind his back.

She couldn't help but empathise.

What did it say about the director's leadership when he was so desperate as to take tips from some random person off the street?

Not that Cassandra was judging.

"All right," Peter said, looking up and smiling. "We'll give it a go."

***

Although Cassandra wasn't quite sure how it happened, she soon found herself standing beside Peter as he gave instructions to his crew. It was surreal to see the page she had sketched out attached to his clipboard, and even more so to see him scrutinising its contents, as if it might hold the secret to some essence he was trying to capture. She wanted to reassure him that she had hardly any experience doing this, and that her suggestions were most likely crap.

But it seemed a shame for her to dampen Peter's enthusiasm when he was clearly having such a good time. As night rolled in over the hills, Peter guided his team along the beach and then up a coastal path, in keeping with her vision.

When they reached the top of the cliff, Cassandra couldn't help but forget the film crew. She was taken by the scene unfolding out ahead. By the sun as its golden rays sparkled off the surface of the water. She watched on as Finn instructed his team about taking the shots while Peter stood a little way back, squinting at the storyboard, and then peering out at the scene beyond. It was almost as if he was waiting for an actor to arrive on set. As if the scene wasn't quite complete. And then Cassandra saw why.

As Finn was speaking with the soundman, Peter cut through their conversation with a wild yelp — something between a bark and a cry of anguish.

Her muscles tightened up. She felt the blood rush about her veins. Her heart beating hard. She wondered if Peter didn't suffer from some form of medical condition, and that now she had dragged them all the way up this cliff he would be rendered in a tricky spot; that she somehow might have had a hand in putting him in danger.

The whole crew turned as one, their expressions stunned.

But she soon saw Peter wasn't in distress.

In fact, he was grinning.

"There, over there," Peter said, his voice throaty, nothing like the sound he had just made. He extended his arm and pointed off to the horizon.

Cassandra looked to where he indicated, realising the sun was sinking in the sky. And that it had turned a gorgeous, intense, grapefruit tone.

Although the crew had clearly been wrapped up in what they had been doing a few seconds ago, they soon shifted their focus — in nimble fashion — to the scene which their director indicated. It was as if anyone speaking might break the effect of the natural display taking place. Cassandra could only draw gasping breaths as she witnessed the birds bobbing in and out of the thermals, as the sun dipped down beneath the horizon for a final time. As night sunk over the landscape.

Only when the sun had totally disappeared did Peter speak to break the silence. "Marvellous," he said, his voice rasping, uneven. "Just *marvellous*."

And it was then that Cassandra caught Finn's eye.

She couldn't help thinking the same.

6

LEAVING PAWLER'S BAY

*C*assandra felt almost as if she had lived a lifetime at Pawler's Bay. She no longer needed convincing — if she ever had done — of the power of simply getting away from day-to-day life. Of how escaping her surroundings afforded her mind the chance to stretch and draw inspiration. It allowed her mind creative freedom again.

As she sat on the edge of her bed, flipping through her sketch-book, she could hardly recall the exact moments when she had created each of the drawings. It was as if they had been mere flickers blown out by a draught as soon as they had crossed her mind's eye and she had committed them to paper.

After looking at her watch, and seeing it was time to catch her train, she packed up the little she had brought with her and checked out of the hotel.

She couldn't help but take another walk along the promenade, take in the beach which stretched out into the sea, and think about the many hours she had spent there. She thought about how quiet things had been, and about how — it being a Friday morning — the beach would soon be crowded with families. That its solitude would be lost. She doubted there would be a more beautiful stretch of days this year.

As she turned her back on the beach, she had the gnawing longing to see Finn for a final time. To look into his eyes. She knew there was nothing real about her stay here. That the whole memory would soon slip into the quicksands of her subconscious. And yet, there still remained the urge for her to see him again.

As she wound her way through the village, in the general direction of the station, she heard a voice calling out. On instinct, she turned upwards, in the direction of the sound. She saw Finn peering down at her from out of a window.

"You're leaving?"

Her pulse quickened. "I'm getting a train."

"Really?"

"Yeah."

With that, his head disappeared.

She had a moment to wonder just what had become of him when a door swung open into the street.

Finn skipped down the steps, his eyes wide, a half smile fixed onto his lips. "Actually," he said, slightly out of breath from his descent. "We were wondering if you might have some more tips for us."

"Oh, it's okay. I already have a job. But thanks."

"No, no — not a job." He eyed her closely then smiled wider. "Unless that's what you'd like." He jerked his thumb over his shoulder. "We just wanted to pick your brain really — you have some local knowledge, don't you?"

"I live in a village about an hour away."

"A village?"

"Yeah."

He clapped his hands together. "Hah! Really?"

"Yes," she replied, repressing the urge to roll her eyes. "There're villages all over this country . . ."

She couldn't help but scold herself. This might well be the final time she would ever see Finn and she was being a snarky bitch.

Finn, however, seemed to brush it off. "Tell me about it."

"Well, it's called Normonswold."

" 'Normonswold' !"

The way Finn phrased it made it sound as if Normonswold was among the greatest jokes ever made in the English language.

"That's right," she continued. "Well, there's nothing all that special about it really." She felt her heart wrench slightly. "There's a forest, a church, and a river . . . a quaint countryside village, really. Lots of cute cottages and not a lot going on."

"But you're there."

A long silence followed.

Her shoulders went tense.

"I mean," Finn went on, running his hands through his hair, suddenly looking flustered, "if you're living there then there must be some sort of charm? Some sort of attraction?"

"Well, it's where my job is."

"Still, it takes some *job* or some *scenery* — or a combination of the two — to drag someone away from human civilisation, don't you think?"

Unsure whether or not Finn wanted to insinuate just what he was insinuating, she replied. "I suppose it does."

"Look, what time's your train?"

She glanced at her watch. "It leaves in ten minutes."

"Are you in a hurry to get back?"

She weighed up the question. Then decided. "Not really. There's another at noon."

He held her gaze. "Look, we've been searching for something 'quaint' . . . somewhere which would be receptive to a film crew turning up."

It was then Cassandra brought to mind Frieda Smyth, the proprietor of the Thicket Arms Inn. She was hardly the most welcoming soul in the world, and that was surely where the film crew would wind up staying. But, all the same, she replied, "I think people would be flattered that you wanted to take footage in Normonswold."

He grinned. "Great — that's great." He turned back, headed up the stairs. "I'll tell the others to pack up and we can head off as soon as possible, okay?"

Feeling a touch giddy, she calmed herself with the sensation of the gentle ocean breeze blowing against the side of her face. As she stood staring out over the sea, absorbing the view for what might be the last time for a long while, she wondered if she had really made the right choice.

If Normonswold really would take a film crew to its heart.

And whether she should really be letting Finn closer to her . . .

7

A FRESH MILIEU

*A*t midday, Cassandra felt strange as she helped the film crew unload their van in the middle of Normonswold Village. Although there was nobody standing by, watching on with curiosity — they would be peeping out of windows — she knew they would already be the talk of the town. Normonslanders were extraordinarily efficient gossips.

Leaving Peter to unload with the rest of his team, Cassandra approached the reception of the Thicket Arms Inn with Finn pacing alongside. Although she had been to the pub at the Thicket Arms Inn more times than she wished to count, she had only been in the reception area of the hotel a handful of times, if that.

There was little doubting that the place was memorable, however.

And 'memorable' was certainly the word.

Several glass cases contained beady-eyed, stuffed birds. And the patterned wallpaper reminded Cassandra of an old persons' home where she had worked back when she'd been a teenager. The whole place had a slight scent of damp and musk, and was so dark that hardly a ray of midday sun managed to penetrate.

She approached the deadpan Frieda Smyth, standing at the desk, and looking somewhat distastefully at the new-arrivals. "No reservation?"

Cassandra gave her a weak smile and thought of Finn's question about whether the Normonslanders would be welcoming. Frieda Smyth was hardly representative of the whole village, though. Cassandra turned on her charm as best she was able. "No, I'm afraid not. Are there any vacancies?"

"What does it look like? Hardly the Ritz at Christmas, is it?"

Cassandra felt a slight twinge in her gut. She was all too aware Finn was standing at her elbow, witnessing the entire conversation. She supposed she could be thankful the rest of the film crew were outside, unloading the van.

Frieda Smyth looked from Cassandra to Finn, and then back again. "I've said it before, but this place isn't a motel, you understand?"

"Excuse me?" Finn said, apparently unable to keep himself from butting in.

Frieda stared razor blades.

Finn — somehow — managed to hold her gaze.

"Well," Frieda said, dropping a key with a *clatter* upon the counter, "I suppose nobody much cares for this village anymore. Not with all these outsiders living here. No sense of the history, see? No sense of traditional values."

Cassandra gritted her teeth. "We'll need two more rooms, please."

Frieda froze Cassandra in her glare. " 'Two more rooms' ?"

"That's right."

If Frieda had been anyone else in the world, Cassandra might've expected an apology, but she knew one would not be forthcoming. Even though there had been something of a thawing of relations between Frieda Smyth and the world — when Kareema Ashburton had visited — she saw things were very much back to normal.

To how they had always been.

With another pair of *clatters*, two more keys landed upon the reception desk.

"That all?" Frieda asked.

"What time's breakfast?" Finn asked.

"Information's all on the notice," she replied, disappearing into the back room.

Finn exchanged a glance with Cassandra, and then the two of them looked at the all-knowing notice. Sure enough, there were all the relevant details.

Check-in time.

Check-*out* time.

Breakfast.

A forewarning about smoking in the rooms, excessive noise, bringing animals other than guide dogs into the hotel, and a pointed, no-nonsense policy about lost property not being the responsibility of the establishment.

In the back room, a TV burbled to life, loud enough to drown out a moderately-sized rock concert.

They got the equipment upstairs without having to encounter Frieda another time. Cassandra had the urge to apologise, but decided it was probably best not to draw attention to the issue.

Finn would've made up his mind, in any case . . . in particular in terms of what it said about the village as a whole.

As Cassandra stood in the doorway to Peter and Finn's room, she prepared a pithy leaving statement. But nothing came to mind. The phone rang and Peter answered. It was clearly an entertaining call, because he burst into fits of laughter several times over before finally bidding the person on the other end a hearty goodbye and replacing the receiver. He turned to Finn and Cassandra grinning. "That was someone called Indigo Miles," he said.

Cassandra felt her stomach turn slightly. "Oh, really, was it?"

"She's heard there's a film crew in town and she would simply *love* to show us her home — a place called Ebundlover, or something?"

"Ebbendevor?"

"Yes, I believe that was it. She says it's the crowning jewel of Normonswold."

Despite feeling Peter and Finn's dual gaze upon her, Cassandra said nothing. She was determined to allow them to make their own mind up . . . to decide whether or not the hype lived up to the reality.

"She's invited us for afternoon tea. Why don't we go and see her right away?"

Again, Cassandra said nothing. She wondered if she should warn them, but decided it would only be in vain. Once Indigo Miles got her claws into something — especially anything which was vaguely glamourous or *spectacular* — it took a very stubborn fool to attempt to prise it away.

Finally, the ability for speech returned to Cassandra. "I was thinking of dropping in at the office on the way, if that's all right? I don't think you'll get lost, though. It's the road leading out of the village. And the house *is* unmissable."

Peter and Finn exchanged glances. She expected Finn to suggest they have some time for relaxation, but he seemed just as keen as Peter to see Ebbendevor. She supposed you didn't get ahead in show business by lying in bed all day.

"Let's go, then," Finn said.

Cassandra took a backward step, out of the room.

Finn's reaction to her attempted retreat was so dramatic it was almost as if she had popped a balloon. "What're your plans this evening?"

"Uh, I'm not sure."

Peter was staring at her too. "We would love to meet for dinner if you are free. I hear — from Finn — that you have a very interesting business venture here, in the village. Greetings cards?"

"Yes, that's right." Cassandra couldn't help but think — by the sound of Peter's tone — he was in for a shock when he discovered just how big Humble Greetings really was. Albeit they seemed like a small operation in Molinaar's Cottage.

"Shall we say six, seven?" Peter asked.

"Yes, that's fine," Cassandra replied, and then, taking another series of backward steps, left the room.

As she ventured out through the reception area, she heard Frieda Smyth give a very pointed cough from within the back room.

8

EBBENDEVOR

*F*inn felt the gentle rumble of the engine through the van steering wheel. He couldn't help but feel the excitement which cut through the group — that same enthusiasm they all shared for discovery . . . for seeing a new place . . . for being the first to document something which hadn't previously, or recently, been documented. It was awe-inspiring to think about the number of hidden jewels there were scattered about the United Kingdom, and Finn couldn't help thinking they were to experience another.

There was something about the name itself which sparked the imagination. There was little doubt about that.

Ebbendevor.

There it was, spelled out on the towering, wrought-iron gates.

A little way beyond, he could see the house growing up and out of the surrounding forests. One of the cameramen got down from the van and opened the gate.

To begin with, as they travelled up the drive, Finn thought they had stumbled across some sort of mausoleum. The house had been freshly daubed in bright white paint so it caught the afternoon sun and shone. As they rounded the bend, all at once, the house had a sense of the homey, the eerie and the romantic. He looked to the mansard roof, and then the tower — the lightning rod poking up to the sky the highest point of the building. He was of a mind to get out of the van and to have the crew commence filming right away . . . but they hadn't even met the house owner yet.

They pulled into the driveway, alongside a hatchback and a larger estate car.

As the crew unloaded equipment, Finn and Peter made their way up the steps to the front door. It was Peter — nodding to Finn — who brought the knocker down. Finn supposed it was only Pete's right, as director, that he should be the one to do the knocking when there was knocking to be done.

They waited for fewer than three seconds before the door swung open. A beaming woman of about sixty stood on the step, staring out at them. She was wearing a pink satin dress beneath which Finn could make out her bare feet. A pearl necklace dangled around her throat. There was an alarmingly strong scent of lavender which puffed up Finn's nostrils, but he managed to hold back his sneeze. "Welcome, welcome!" she said, in a sing-song voice, standing to one side to allow them in.

Finn nodded to Peter, and Peter crossed the threshold.

———

The interior of the house lived up to the approach.

In the front hall, there was an expansive slate floor, with a chandelier hanging from the ceiling. Not that there was much time to appreciate this as Indigo Miles led them deeper into her labyrinth.

They ended up in a modern converted kitchen. Finn was surprised about how much sun got into the room. About how in a house as old as this someone had given thought to the lighting of the kitchen. Then again, in his childhood, Finn's mother had always been fussy about the condition of her kitchen, and it was no wonder really, seeing she had spent a great amount of time there baking treats for him and his father.

His mother would've loved the kitchen's brilliant lighting, that was for certain.

Indigo Miles waved her arm wildly about the kitchen table and Finn took this as his cue to sit. He did so. And Peter followed.

Before either of them had any say in the matter, the kettle was boiling and Indigo Miles had flipped into full-on interrogation mode.

"So, this *film*," she began, "is it to be shown in cinemas?"

Peter blew on his tea, sending up a scalding cloud of steam. "TV."

Finn sat back, surprised they were even *drinking* tea on such a fine afternoon. He would've been glad to accept a glass of cold fruit juice, or even a beer, if there had been one going.

"Ah," Indigo replied, sounding somewhat disappointed. "A TV film, then?"

Again, Peter shook his head. "Documentary. The footage we're shooting is going to be used to supplement the main feature."

"I see," Indigo said, eyeing Finn suspiciously. Then, as if she had just had a colossal realisation, she slapped her forehead and her mouth gaped open like a banked fish. "Goodness, I forgot to ask if you take sugar!"

Finn forced a smile. "No, no sugar for me, thanks."

"Ah, I am glad." Clearly versed in how to deal with hierarchies of power, she switched her attention back to Peter. "And where exactly would pictures of Ebbendevor — *my home* — be featured in this TV programme?"

"Well," Peter began, eyeing Finn, "in the main feature, the presenters will be travelling about the country, making stops as they go. When they move from one place to another, there will be footage of the countryside — you know, of the greenery, and of the villages they all pass through, things like that?"

Finn couldn't help but feel greatly uneasy about the expression which had now appeared on Indigo's face, and he wanted nothing more than to be able to send Peter a subtle message that he should *STOP TALKING NOW.*

However, it was too late.

Indigo Miles cocked her head to one side. "You mean it's a *fraud?*"

" 'A fraud' ?" Peter echoed, as if he had no idea what the word meant. "No, no . . . things are always done this way. It's how they give programmes a grander depth. It's the most efficient way of doing things."

"But it's a lie?" Indigo said, looking to Finn now. "I mean, these presenters are representing that they are going to *all* of these places, and they never actually go to them. They just send a crew — like yours — and use the footage as part of their final programme?"

Finn had to work hard to keep himself from nodding in response to this — to keep from acknowledging that this was, in fact, the case. He performed some minor miracle in breaking off the stare Indigo was subjecting him to, looking across the table at Peter, attempting to pass the buck.

Peter had turned a deep shade of red, and he was blinking

rapidly, sure-fire signs that he was flustered by the line of ques-
tioning . . . or that anybody would have taken his explanation for
the Way Things Were as anything other than perfectly reasonable
— entirely consistent with logic. "Well, yes," Peter finally said. "We
are supplementing the main film team. You do realise, do you not,
that films are shot in a non-linear fashion? That any scene which
doesn't involve showing an actor or presenter's face might well
have been shot at any given moment?"

From Indigo's tight-lipped expression, it seemed that she
did not.

If Finn had been able to reach, he might've given Peter a kick in
the shins.

Indigo stood at the kitchen counter, staring at her bare toes for
several seconds, and Finn couldn't help the tightening sensation in
his chest — an uncomfortable feeling similar to the one of telling a
child that Father Christmas didn't exist.

"No, I didn't realise that," Indigo replied, finally. Then, with a
sigh, she peeled herself away from the kitchen counter. She
pressed on a smile, then said, "Well, I suppose I should give you a
tour of the house, should I not? Give you an idea about what might
work with the film the *other* crew is shooting?"

Finn glanced down at his untouched tea. He wondered if he
should attempt to down it in one, but decided against it. In any
case, it didn't appear Indigo Miles was all that interested in
whether or not he drank it now.

9

EVENING PLANS

"*W*hat're you so happy about?" Bella said.

Cassandra turned away from her mirror, where she had been working to prod an earring through her earlobe. When she looked to her bedroom doorway, she saw Bella leaning there. She had arrived so silently that Cassandra was concerned about just how long she had been watching her. Then again, she supposed it was her own fault for not closing the door in the first place. Robert's dog Woss was at Bella's heels. His tongue was lolling about the side of his mouth as he dealt with the humid heat which'd moved in with the cloud cover this evening. It had to be that Robert was out somewhere, because otherwise Woss would've been at his master's side. It was only when Robert wasn't in that Woss took to following Bella everywhere.

" 'Happy' ?" Cassandra replied. "I'm not really happy about anything . . ." But she could feel the smile bursting off her lips, the hop in her voice as she spoke.

"What's his name?"

"Whose name?"

"*His* name." Bella twirled her fingers impatiently. "This man of your dreams."

"There is no man of my dreams. The man of my dreams is the muse which drives my impatient pencil — which draws wonders from my subconscious . . . and which keeps us all fed and sheltered, etcetera, etcetera . . ."

Bella remained serious for another second, then cracked a grin.

Cassandra's smile widened, too.

Bella took this as her invitation to enter. She perched on the edge of Cassandra's bed. Woss held back reverently another few moments, and then trotted inside, entirely unaware that this was a conversation unsuited to male ears.

"It was at the bay, wasn't it?" Bella asked. "That's where you met him. He's one of the guys in the film crew you brought back, is he not?" She snapped her fingers. "I knew there had to be a reason you brought them home!"

Taken off guard by the rush of questions, Cassandra glanced about, as if the film crew was going to come marching through Molinaar's cottage itself. "I . . . don't know."

Bella rolled her eyes. "You don't *know*?"

"I mean," Cassandra went on, "I wasn't the one who asked them to come back to Normonswold — they kind of proposed things to me . . . I was going to get the train. I was going to come back alone, like I had planned it . . ."

"But you didn't."

Cassandra bowed her head to hide her blushes.

Bella sighed and then arched an eyebrow. "My mother's already got her claws into them, you'll be glad to know. It won't be long before we know what they're really made of . . ."

Cassandra was unsure what to do with this piece of information, so she remained silent. She half hoped something might distract Bella — that the phone might begin to ring, or that Harriet and George would show up at the front door with some important news. But, as always seemed to be the case, whenever Cassandra most wished for an interruption, there was none to be found. Even as Cassandra sat under Bella's watchful gaze, though, she could feel her mind slipping back to Finn. About how she had first seen him on the beach at the bay. It had been like a dream, or maybe it had simply been the sea air getting to her. "I don't know *how* to feel," Cassandra finally found herself saying.

"So which one is it?" Bella's expression went stern all of a sudden. "Not the director — the sixty-year-old guy?"

"No! Not him."

Bella shrugged then smiled, somewhat sheepishly. "I dunno, thought I'd better ask. I've never seen you involved with anyone. Not really sure what your type is."

"I don't have a type."

"Of course you do . . . *everybody* does."

"Then I don't know what it is."

"You know it when you see it."

Here Cassandra realised she had nothing more to say — that Bella had caught her down some sort of a dead-end. She looked to Woss, as if he was going to give them some sort of a conversational way-out. However, when Bella spoke again, it was only to announce that events had taken a turn for the worse.

"My mother has invited us — the whole Humble Greetings crew — to Ebbendevor for the evening." Bella set Cassandra in an intense glare, in imitation of her mother. "You don't have plans, do you?"

"I just got back!"

"But you have no plans?"

Cassandra thought about how she had said to Finn she would meet the film crew — or had it just been him? — for dinner that evening. Surely that qualified as a plan?

"And before you mumble something about seeing to the boys — or rather *boy* — in the film crew, I must inform you that they have been catered for. They too, will be dining at Ebbendevor this evening."

Cassandra felt the last of her hope slide away.

Bella straightened herself up, and Woss mimicked her, rising up off his haunches. Bella stretched her arms to the ceiling, unknotting herself from the position she had been sitting in. "So, you see, dear Cass, there really is no way out. You would do much better to come along quietly. It would be much less *painful* for you."

Cassandra sank onto the stool before her makeup mirror.

She had absolutely *nothing* to wear.

10

EBBENDEVOR AT NIGHT

hen Cassandra arrived on the front steps of Ebbendevor, with Robert, Bella, George and Harriet in tow, she felt somewhat uneasy. Perhaps it was the ruby-red ball gown which Bella had dressed her in. Maybe it was the moonlight which shone through the trees, making everything seem unreal, as if produced by some sort of spectral projector.

Cassandra couldn't help feeling that Bella had conspired with Harriet to dress themselves down, so that Cassandra would stand out. And Cassandra always felt uncomfortable whenever she stood out — she had always made an effort to blend into the background. There would be little prospect of blending into the background tonight, though. Even Robert's dog Woss was wearing a bowtie.

It was Dorothy who greeted them at the door, wearing a dress of his own. He grinned at them as he waved them inside. Cassandra made a point of being the last to step over the threshold. As she went in, Dorothy whispered to her.

"Guess the trip was worth it after all."

Cassandra felt herself blushing beneath the many layers of makeup which Bella had subjected her to. She concentrated on putting one foot in front of the other — in not tripping up over herself. Bella led the way, taking them through the winding corridors with which she was so familiar.

They made for the dining room — where Cassandra recalled Indigo Miles entertaining Lord Charles . . . if 'entertain' was the right word to use.

The dining table was set for fourteen, which accommodated the film crew, the Humble Greetings team, Indigo Miles, and Dorothy. As Cassandra looked about the room, she realised a dog bed had been placed in the corner. Woss — not one to waste a second when he saw a chance for rest and/or relaxation — made for it immediately.

"The boys are just washing up," Indigo Miles said, appearing in the doorway which led to the kitchen and startling Cassandra a little. "They'll be turning up any minute."

Cassandra took stock of Indigo Miles. Tonight, she was wearing a satiny, silver-white dress which showed off the delicate skin at her throat. Her gaze ploughed over the whole group, absorbing absolutely everything. Cassandra couldn't help but notice she lingered for a particularly long time on her. It took Cassandra a moment to realise that this was because she approved of her appearance rather than had some sort of complaint. Cassandra wasn't sure whether or not she should take Indigo's approval as a good or bad thing . . . it was as if her card had been marked, pending future judgement.

She took her place at the table, sitting with the rest of the Humble Greetings team. It was on nights like these when Cassandra had learned the true extent of Indigo Mile's powers —

how she was capable of not only dressing herself so divinely, but also of taking charge of the kitchen, of tending to the assembled guests as if she had a permanent house staff. Tonight, she was ably assisted by Dorothy, who rushed back and forth at Indigo's every will and whim.

While they waited for the others to arrive, Indigo served them each a glass of white wine. As the others fell into easy conversation about the day's activities at Humble — about some deal George and Harriet had struck with an overseas distributor — Cassandra couldn't help but feel herself falling further and further away. It was like she was sinking into an oily pit, slowly becoming more and more distant from the real world, gradually sinking deeper and deeper. It was times like these she had the urge to lock herself away somewhere and sketch for hours on end.

But there was no prospect of that at present.

No, she had to be *sociable*.

The only warning of the film crew's arrival were the woody thunks on the front door, accompanied by Indigo's excited shriek, and her order for Dorothy to go and let the guests in. Cassandra sucked in her gut and sipped at her white wine, anticipating the dinner to come.

Peter — the director — had truly outdone himself. He was wearing a three-piece tuxedo.

Bella spoke up first. "I didn't realise a tux was a standard piece of kit for the travelling film crew?"

"My dear," Peter replied, "when you are involved in the movie business, you need to be prepared for anything." He took a seat. "You never know when you might be called away to attend this party, or that . . . *awards* ceremony."

Cassandra wasn't quite sure exactly what Peter meant to

communicate in emphasising 'awards' so fervently. Perhaps it was because he had never been given one.

The others, it had to be said, looked altogether more rag-tag.

Finn included, they all wore a collection of half-crumpled — clearly hastily ironed — shirts which were tucked into dark-toned trousers, the material of which ranged from jeans, to chino, to something which Cassandra really wouldn't have liked to hazard a guess at . . .

They all took their places hurriedly, perhaps concerned they might be tossed out on their ear if Indigo had the chance of casting her discerning eye over them before they were seated. Indeed, when Indigo did appear once more, a momentary scowl crossed her expression, only abating when she settled upon Peter.

"Why, Peter! You look simply *divine!*"

Peter flushed slightly at this remark, and he hurried up to his feet so he might be on the receiving end of Indigo's kiss on each cheek.

Once Peter had resettled himself at the table, looking somewhat ruffled in his pristinely turned-out tuxedo, Indigo addressed the other members of the film crew, her smile dialling itself down several notches in intensity. "And you all look . . . lovely — who would've known that a group of adventurers could scrub up so effectively."

Cassandra cast a glance in Finn's direction, and was surprised to find he was staring right back at her. She felt a warm sensation shimmer through her stomach, and turned away to regard Woss, sleeping soundly in the corner.

Once the first glass of wine had been consumed, conversation began to flow much more freely, mostly instigated by Peter's — admittedly hilarious — accounts of the various filming jobs he had worked on. Cassandra surprised even herself that she was having a good time in the company of others. When Indigo and Dorothy served them dessert, Peter was as good as the host. Perhaps Indigo had had far more foresight than Cassandra had credited her with since she had sat him at the head of the table. Sitting with his head cocked, Peter admired the chocolate soufflé. He spoke in a stage whisper.

"Goodness, what a wonderful way to finish another tour of duty."

Indigo — just taking her seat across from him — did not miss out on this statement. "Oh, you're leaving Normonswold? And so soon?"

Cassandra felt a stab in her chest, and she looked over at Finn, with something of an accusatorial stare. Finn continued to examine his soufflé, picking at it with his spoon.

"Well, that's the game," Peter continued. "I travel to work, in every sense of the phrase." He smiled at himself. "I have never really settled anywhere, and I suppose I'm too old for the habit to die now."

Indigo leaned over the table, her spoon clutched between her fingers, the soufflé forgotten. "Don't you have a home — somewhere to go back to?

Peter gave a shrug. "Well, yes, I have a *house* . . . but I wouldn't term it my *home* as such. Given, all my possessions are there, and it is where I must spend the majority of my time when I'm not on the road. There's no sentimental attachment, though. I suppose that is what I wanted to get across."

He had certainly got that point across to Cassandra, and she couldn't help wondering just exactly what his motive was in playing this card so vociferously.

"Well," Indigo replied, settling back into her seat, regaining her composure, "you shall always be most welcome here, in Normonswold. On one condition."

"What's that?" Peter asked.

"That the thought of staying in the *fleapit* that is the Thicket Arms Inn never again crosses your mind. Is that clear?"

Peter was grinning now. "Absolutely."

Once dinner was over with, Cassandra expected Indigo to make some gesture which would release them all from the invitation. A yawn, or a sigh. But nothing of the sort came about. She remained just as energised as ever. Perhaps it was down to the coffee which she had prepared to accompany the soufflé.

As conversation fell to a hush — with even Peter's almighty stock of war stories seemingly well exploited — Indigo clapped her hands together.

"Dancing!"

Cassandra was taken aback for a moment, unsure if she had quite heard correctly. It was feasible Indigo had slipped into a foreign language — some stylish French phrase which had simply passed her by. In any case, she had no need to request clarification, because Bella stepped in.

"Dancing, mother?"

Indigo's eyes blazed and she grinned. "Yes — *dancing!*" It was now that she got up from her chair and did a spontaneous pirouette. Before anybody could say anything further, she had crossed the dining room, and disappeared through the doorway. After about half a minute, there was the scratching of a needle locating a groove in vinyl, and a waltz kicked in.

Cassandra felt a surge of panic. She looked about the table, hoping someone might have a plan. However, everyone was rendered just as startled by Indigo's declaration.

Breaking into a grin to rival Indigo's, Dorothy rose from his seat, and declared, in a booming, *unfeminine* voice, "*Dancing!*" and disappeared too.

Cassandra knew she was quickly coming across the final opportunity to cut and run. They had all arrived in cars so as not to ruin their elegant outfits on the short but muddy walk from Normonswold to Ebbendevor. She could conceivably make her way back home along the road, but it would be the end for her dress. And she would forever have a black mark against her name in Indigo Miles's books.

Peter finally got to his feet, and with a sheepish smile, made his way through the same doorway. Next up, it was Harriet and George, who exchanged a shrug and followed on Peter's heels. Bella and Robert weren't far behind, though Cassandra did her level best to catch Bella's eye, hoping to silently communicate her need for a fast excuse to get out of this mess. But it was in vain. Soon enough, it was Cassandra alone with Finn and the other four members of the film crew. One of the cameramen addressed Finn.

"Think we're gonna make a break for it, if that's all right with you?"

Finn held himself still, then glanced to Cassandra, as if she held any sort of sway over tonight's comings and goings. He seemed to give up on this soon enough, turning back to the film crew. He shrugged. "Sure, guys, do whatever you want."

"All right if we take the van?"

"Uh" — Finn dug about in his pocket, produced the key, then handed it over — "here you go."

The film crew wasted no time in beating it out of the dining room. This left Finn and Cassandra alone together. With the sound of the waltz in the background, Cassandra realised she could finally speak with him in peace.

"You're not much of a dancer, are you?" she said.

Finn smirked then shook his head. "No, are you?"

"I think it'd be in everyone's best interests that we *don't* go next door — I don't want to put anybody's eye out."

"Agreed. Better if nobody ends up in hospital after such a lovely night."

Cassandra got up from where she sat. "I assume you've already had a substantial tour of Ebbendevor — Indigo doesn't allow anybody to leave without them having been thoroughly acquainted with the house."

"I wouldn't assume anything at this point."

"Did you see the garden?"

"Would it be terrible to lie and say I haven't?"

A smile tweaked Cassandra's lips. "All right, let's start there."

***

Outside, the air was pleasantly cool. Cassandra imagined that — upon first hearing there was a film crew in town — Indigo had called up her gardener to get to work trimming the bushes and mowing the lawn. The effect was the perfect scene opening up ahead, lit with electric lights scattered about flowerbeds like fireflies. The moon shone, giving everything a kind of ethereal tone.

Before Cassandra could really take stock of what was going on, she felt Finn take gentle hold of her elbow. She quivered slightly at his touch, but didn't resist. After the first moment of panic had dissipated, she relaxed into him.

"Is this the best way?" Finn asked, indicating the stone slabs lying on the lawn and leading into the trees which ran alongside the garden.

"I suppose it's the way Indigo wants people to experience her home."

"Then it'd be rude not to follow."

Cassandra removed the high heels Bella had instructed her to wear, and then, bare-footed, allowed Finn to lead the way, taking them away from the house, and into the trees. She breathed in the overwhelming scent of the rose bushes, and of the mint and lavender. There was something refreshing about the garden here, and she could almost *feel* the years of love and affection which Indigo had invested in Ebbendevor.

Would she one day own a home of her own with a similar sort of personal weight attached? Was that what she wanted?

As they ventured deeper into the foliage, it was like she was leaving the world behind — as if she and Finn were stepping out onto a whole new plane.

It was then that Finn paused their advance.

The moon glimmering between the branches made Finn's eyes glint, and his black hair sheen. She felt her heart bob in her throat.

His lips pressed up against hers.

Warm.

Soft.

Slightly moist.

She sank into him gradually but surely. She seemed to be departing from her body . . . rising up in the air.

And yet Finn kept her grounded.

He stopped her floating away.

As they moved apart again, the moon set Finn in the fore-ground. There was just one thought which came to mind — the words tumbled out between her lips.

"Is it true you're leaving?"

Finn held himself still. "Filming's over. We're running a tight schedule. One day is about all we can spare."

"You didn't answer the question."

"Are you saying I should stay here, in Normonswold?"

Cassandra held herself very still — a grand feat seeing as she felt her whole body trembling. She focused upon Finn once more. "I'm not saying anything — I'm just asking."

11

BACK TO WORK

*F*inn woke the next morning feeling as if he was wrapped in cotton wool. Blood pulsed about his body. The sun shimmering through the curtains seemed like the most beautiful sight he had ever laid his eyes upon, and he hardly noticed Peter's snoring from the bed alongside his. He rose, showered, then wolfed down breakfast. He was glad to find it was a self-service buffet and that there was no need for interaction with the proprietor — Frieda Smyth. That done, he donned his long coat and stepped outside, venturing along the main street of Normonswold.

It was incredible to consider this place. It was nothing less than a fully realised rendering of what appeared in his mind's eye when he thought of an Idyllic Countryside Village. Almost too true to believe, really. And the sort of place he had expended energy rallying himself to avoid. His had been a life of adventure, of travelling the world, of documenting that which he felt compelled to document.

And now, standing in a small town in England, he felt a shimmer pass across the surface of his skin. As if there was something within him which physically repelled the 'charms' of such a place. He saw this for what it was, an artists' retreat, a sleepy retirement location . . . not the kind of place where any sort of real *culture* went to flourish. And yet, who was he to anoint himself the bastion of 'culture'? Could he really say that the works he had produced over the years would stand any sort of test of time? All of these half-arsed TV programmes, documentaries, and short films. He supposed his greatest ever achievement had been in directing what could optimistically be referred to as a 'sleeper hit' which had gone on to win some minor awards.

But even that had been five, six years ago.

Was he past his peak?

As he continued along the street, he found himself going past Molinaar's Cottage — where Cassandra lived, and the unassuming HQ of Humble Greetings. He wondered just how any sort of business could expect to thrive on any kind of international level operating from a place such as this. Surely Humble would need to relocate if all the stories of grand success he had overheard from Indigo Miles were correct . . . then again, he supposed that Indigo, being the mother of one of the founders, was liable to exaggerate — especially when in the presence of outsiders, soon to move on, and less likely to make enquiries as to the authenticity of such claims. Finn knew first-hand that his own mother was his number one fan — the first to cheer on any of his successes, and — more frequently — to downplay the failures.

He passed Molinaar's Cottage.

God, it was difficult to believe places like Normonswold even existed.

And yet, here was the living proof.

When he reached the end of the village — the place where the road led to Ebbendevor —he stopped and turned around.

He took in the village ahead of him, spread out.

Every logical impulse compelled him to get away.

To go somewhere else.

There was so much more to be discovered.

And yet . . . and yet there was something which tied him here.

Which would not allow him to leave.

Had it been last night?

Was Cassandra — already — that important to him?

To make him give up on his dreams . . . to stay here . . .

Or was it something still deeper, some survival instinct nudging him, informing him he had reached the end of the road? That he was about to repeat the familiar tale which had dominated his career to date.

Another project.

Another chain of weeks.

Another *disappointment*.

He could do a lot worse than stay in Normonswold . . .

Wasn't he overdue a chance to 'find himself'?

His mind returned to Cassandra.

Just the thought of her stoked a fire in his stomach.

It made him anxious.

Uncomfortable, almost.

But perhaps he had been too comfortable — perhaps he needed to step outside his comfort zone.

Perhaps he did need to stay in Normonswold a while.

12

SKETCHBOOK

*S*un streamed through the windows of the studio at Molinaar's Cottage. There were a few fluffy clouds in the distance and Cassandra wondered if they would bring rain in the afternoon — there was certainly the smell of it in the air. She brought the studio door shut behind her, and slid the lock into place.

Although she and Bella shared the same studio, they had made a rule early on that if either of them wished for some privacy in their work, they were only to slide the lock into place. Cassandra had only executed this right on a couple of other occasions, but this — somehow — seemed like another appropriate one.

Unlike so many others, Bella shared Cassandra's understanding of the importance of being away from the world a while. The importance of taking some time out from the constant overflow of incoming sensations.

She slid the sketchbook she had taken with her to Pawler's Bay from where she had tucked it beneath her arm, and laid it down upon her the desk.

She peeled back the pages, her eyes skittering across the drawings. This was the first time she had actually had a chance to look over her work with any sort of a critical eye. As it was with all of her work, as she looked over the sketches she had created, she was brought into mind of all the things which'd happened around those moments. The sounds of gulls cackling, the sweep of the tide upon the rocks, and the feel of the sea breeze blowing against her cheeks. It was as if she was back at Pawler's Bay once again.

As if she had got away from Normonswold once more.

While she looked over the pages, she thought of the time she had spent with the film crew — the time she had spent with Finn.

On instinct, she glanced up, turning her attention to the street outside. It was like something unfurling from a dream. She watched on as Finn — dressed in a long jacket — strolled by on the opposite side. He didn't look back to Molinaar's Cottage. Before she knew it, he had slipped from sight.

Cassandra had the strongest urge to get up, to burst forth from Molinaar's Cottage, to pursue Finn down the road.

What if she never saw him again?

What if that was the last time she saw him?

He hadn't given her a straight answer when she had asked him whether he was going to leave Normonswold with the rest of the film crew, and although her logical mind couldn't help but think there could be no other explanation — that there was nothing tying him to this place — her girlish fantasies were playing tricks upon her; as they almost always seemed to do.

She wanted him to stay.

After about five minutes of thinking of nothing much at all, she turned back to her sketchbook. As with all of her work in this stage, she thought of it as being amateurish, lacking finesse. But she had time to refine what she had had in mind — she could invest the required effort in giving it the glimmer which she recognised as being her 'style' . . .

As being the Humble Greetings 'style'.

She produced several blank pages from a drawer and laid them upon the desk. As she worked through the sketchbook, she took small details and then began to improvise around them. With Humble Greetings, she and Bella had made a point of making things as minimalist as possible. The words were few, and the drawings were always far more suggestive than descriptive.

She started out with the coastline, using it as a backdrop for a silent scene.

Pleased with how it had worked out, she placed this page to one side, turning onto the seagulls flapping through the air, rendering another few designs based on them.

It almost felt too easy.

She felt like a fraud more often than not.

The system she had worked out was to produce a pile of ideas and to make Bella responsible for picking out the ones which would feature on greetings cards. Even though Bella very often selected the same designs Cassandra herself favoured.

This made Cassandra feel more of an *authentic* artist.

To have someone *curate* her work.

And it warded off the feeling that somebody was buying up all of the greetings cards just to please her. That somebody wanted to *make* her believe that she was a real artist, when — in reality — she was nothing more than a phony.

It was times like these that she tried to picture herself back when she had been a teenager. When she had returned home from school and sealed herself off in her bedroom, and just *drawn* because that had been what she had felt compelled to do. There was no need to feel exposed to teachers' questions in classrooms, or to make believe she was at ease in the company of her schoolmates.

She hadn't needed to please anybody else.

Only herself.

Now, though, there was more than just herself to please.

Sometimes she would have dreams about faceless crowds, expanding out to the horizon. All of those people who bought the greetings cards . . . all of those who looked to her, and to Bella, to provide inspiration for messages they wished to deliver to friends and loved ones. What if they decided her sketches no longer represented their feelings?

What if everyone — *all at once* — decided Humble Greetings had nothing to offer?

It was then she felt as if an overwhelming, invisible weight pressed down upon her shoulders. Her whole body began to tremble. She felt faint. When she turned to look at the pile of drawings she had produced — the ones she had extrapolated from the sketchbook she had taken with her to the bay — she saw nothing of value. She saw no end to whatever she had hoped to produce. She saw only demented, twisted renderings.

Why wouldn't the drawings come out the right way?

The walls squeezed in on all sides.

Her heart thumped in her throat.

It was difficult to breathe.

Only vaguely conscious, she rose to her feet, her chair falling to the floor.

She needed some distance.

She needed to . . . *get away* . . .

And yet she had just come back.

She had only just returned.

Cassandra was fortunate there was nobody in the kitchen. Only Woss slumbering away on his doggy bed in the corner, and he was hardly going to give her away. She thought about sneaking upstairs to her bedroom, and packing some clothes, but decided it was too risky. That she might run into Bella on the way out . . . and she wasn't certain she would be able to pretend. That she would be able to *fake* that she was okay.

Sometimes it was so difficult to smile.

Once she made it out of the front door, she set a sure pace along the street. She had no destination in mind — only the idea she should get away from Normonswold as quickly as possible.

That she should get away from the pressure as quickly as possible.

Storm clouds loomed overhead, and there was a certain silence which draped itself over the village, like a warm, damp cloth. Last night in the garden with Finn seemed so far away now. It was an episode which'd played out in someone else's life.

In some other time entirely.

There was nothing but the present now.

And it weighed her down.

She made it out of the village, and began to walk along the countryside road, leading away from Normonswold for good. Already, she felt better. She felt the weight lifting off her shoulders. Her mind was moving to practicalities. She was thinking about how she would find a room to rent back in the City, and how she would return to her old life. And how nobody would ever know how to find her.

She could have her anonymity again.

Her freedom from responsibility.

It was simple.

Just one foot following the other.

As a few spots of rain began to fall, she realised she could hear the rumble of an engine. On instinct, she turned around, expecting to see the van carrying the film crew away from Normonswold making progress up the road. But she soon realised the sound wasn't coming from behind, but from out ahead.

She weighed up her options. There was a ditch at either side of the road. That was the only possible place for her to hide. But even suffering from whatever wild mood had grabbed her, she saw enough sense to stand her ground.

She stood side-on, preparing to allow the car to pass her by, as was the way when walking the countryside roads surrounding Normonswold. But, even though she kept her gaze averted, her eyes concentrating on the toes of her shoes, she sensed the car slowing as it drew up alongside her.

Before she knew it, she heard a familiar voice.

"Cass? What're you doing out here? It's going to tip it down."

Cassandra knew who it was without even needing to look up.

Harriet.

When she did look, she saw Harriet at the wheel, and that George was in the passenger seat beside her. The two of them were in their business wear; the clothing they donned for important meetings — Harriet in a dress, George in a suit.

"I was just . . . going for a walk," Cassandra finally managed to get out.

But she felt herself beginning to crumble.

Why had this happened?

Why hadn't she been given a clear break?

71

She had almost escaped!

The engine still idling, she heard a door open. George appeared at her side, his face twisted in a smile. "Come on," he said, holding out his hand. "Let's get back to Normonswold."

Her heart beat harder still. She could feel her resolve giving way. She knew even before she'd set foot outside the cottage that her confidence would be fragile, that she would need to stick by her intention or else find it quashed beneath the weight of the world. There were those who would be determined to stand in the way of what she wanted — of what she *needed* — to feel like herself again.

"I . . . *can't* . . ."

Even though she didn't bother to look up, she could tell Harriet and George were exchanging glances. That they were attempting to silently divine just what was wrong with her. If they had asked directly, she would've been only too pleased to tell them.

That everything she worked on turned to crap.

That her whole life was a steaming pile of *shit*.

"Let's go, Cass," Harriet said, from behind the steering wheel. "You'll catch a cold out here when it starts to rain."

It was as Cassandra was trying to hold herself together — as she was trying to keep things under control — that she saw a golden glimmer at the very fringes of her vision. She thought it might be the sun.

She knew there was no other option.

That she had been apprehended.

She looked to George and then to Harriet, feeling not a little like a maniac who'd just escaped from an insane asylum. "Okay," she said, and slid into the back seat.

13

EXPLANATIONS

*W*hen Cassandra returned to Molinaar's Cottage, she expected Robert and Bella to be waiting — Harriet and George having surreptitiously alerted them that Cassandra wasn't in her right mind. However, she was surprised to find the house in the exact same state it had been in when she had left not more than an hour ago. Then again, she supposed it *had* only been an hour . . .

The only thing which'd changed in her absence was that Woss was no longer fast asleep on his doggy bed. He had plodded off elsewhere.

Cassandra sat herself down at the kitchen table and allowed Harriet to put on the kettle, and then to serve her tea. Harriet and George seemed tentative about saying anything at all. Cassandra eyed the two of them.

"It's all right," she said, with a slight smile. "You're not going to set me off on some murderous rampage, or anything."

Harriet and George chuckled nervously, but their smiles never got beyond their lips.

Cassandra peered into her tea, considering its murky depths. There had been a time — back when she had had time to spare — that she had sat and stared at any given object; just allowing her mind to get away from her, to form whatever it felt like forming. After a while, her subconscious mind threw her ideas she never could've dreamed of . . . and that would get her sketching. That was when she had had some sense of self-awareness about what she did — some sense of self-awareness about her art. Now, though, it was just an extension of her body.

It wasn't merely *inside* of her.

It *was* her.

In the end, she was glad when Harriet broke the tension, asking the obvious question. "Where were you going, Cass?"

Cassandra smiled again, then, still staring into her tea, shook her head. "Back to the City."

"And you were planning to walk the whole way?"

"No . . . I don't know . . . it seemed like . . . I don't know . . . I needed to get away for a while . . ."

George spoke this time. "But you just came back from holiday."

Cassandra glanced up long enough from her cup of tea to see Harriet firing George a death glare. George quickly took the hint and fled the kitchen, leaving Harriet and Cassandra alone.

Harriet took a seat at the table, beside Cassandra. She hesitated a moment, her cup of tea steaming away. Then she reached out and took hold of Cassandra's hand.

Intertwined their fingers.

When she looked into Harriet's eyes she realised she was crying.

That surprised her.

"It's been a big year, hasn't it?"

Cassandra felt her face grow warm. She could feel a slight prickling sensation at the edges of her eyes. A lump forming in her throat. But she was determined to hold herself together. She wasn't going to crack up for *anybody*.

Harriet went on. "I've done things that . . . well, I never believed myself possible of doing." Another few tears snaked down her cheeks. She wiped them away. "A large part of it has been because of George — because I've had him *pushing* me . . . but another reason, another reason, has just been because I've *wanted* to make changes. That I've put the effort into changing how things were. I . . . know exactly what I would be doing if Bella had never offered me the opportunity of working with Humble — I would have found a job in some office, somewhere, doing the same thing I've always done . . . never challenging myself, always feeling as if there was something missing . . ."

Cassandra met Harriet's eye briefly, and then looked away. "I . . . don't want to sound insensitive, or anything, but is this supposed to relate to me?"

Harriet's tone hardened, becoming brittle almost to the point of breaking. "Comfort zones. We all have to push through them. We have to *keep* on pushing them . . . otherwise we stay in the same place."

"And you think . . . that I'm in my comfort zone?"

Harriet sniffed a half laugh through her tears. "No, but I think you're trying to get *back* to your comfort zone, whatever that place is . . ."

It was then Cassandra realised she could hear footsteps on the staircase. When she turned to look, she saw Bella standing in the doorway.

"Did I miss much?" she asked.

As always, Bella looked effortlessly elegant. She wore a white blouse, and a pair of worn-in jeans. On instinct, Cassandra looked to her left hand, to the little smudge of blue ink which gave away the fact that Bella had been scribbling away somewhere — creating more Humble Greetings. Bella took up a chair at the table, ushering Harriet back into her seat when she rose up to make Bella a cup of tea.

"We were just talking about comfort zones," Cassandra said, in a deadpan voice.

"Ah," Bella said, "I see."

Still in her dress, and surely wanting nothing more than to slip into something more comfortable — and perhaps take a long hot bath — Harriet rolled her shoulders and rubbed the back of her neck. "And I was just telling Cass how important it has been for me, you know, to escape my own comfort zones. To do different things. To take chances. To throw caution to the wind. Blah-tee blah."

"And what brought this on?" Bella asked.

"Me and George caught Cass running away."

" 'Running away' ?" Bella arched an eyebrow and smirked. "Seriously?"

Under any other circumstances — in any other company — Cassandra might've taken this to be in a mocking tone. But she felt comfortable with Harriet and Bella. She was happy for them to have their say. And, what was more, hearing what she had attempted expressed in words made it sound just as ridiculous as it had surely been.

"I was going back to the City," Cassandra said, feeling like a broken record.

Bella extended her look of faux shock. "And just what was waiting for you in the *City*? Another business opportunity you haven't made your partner aware of? You didn't even give me the chance to make a counter offer."

Cassandra felt herself smile. "Nothing's in the City . . . it was just the only place I could think of where I could, you know . . . *disappear?*"

Bella exchanged glances with Harriet. "I see we're getting somewhere now." She shifted back to Cassandra. " 'Disappear' ? Now why would you want to 'disappear' ?"

"I . . ." Cassandra thought through her response, wondering what she could get away with. In the end, she decided she was better off just laying everything out as plainly as she could. "I'm afraid of not being able to do my part for Humble . . . I'm afraid of letting us all down."

There was silence in the kitchen. It was somewhat different to the reaction Cassandra had expected. She had thought Harriet and Bella would laugh the suggestion out of the room all at once. But, no . . .

Bella breathed deeply, clearly thinking through the matter for herself. As she spoke, she addressed the backs of her hands. "It's a legitimate fear. That's the nature of market forces — beyond our control. Anybody's control, really."

Cassandra felt her chest tighten.

"Let me ask you this," Bella continued. "If — for whatever reason — our cards stopped selling, how would you know it was down to your artwork and not my words?"

"I imagine Robert has a way of doing it," Cassandra replied.

Bella smiled. "He probably *thinks* he does, but absolutely nothing is definite. Even he'll tell you there is no knowing one-hundred-percent for sure."

Although Cassandra felt as though she was being led along a path designed to make her feel better, she couldn't help but feel a slight warmth glowing in the pit of her gut. In truth, it didn't matter all that much what Bella or Harriet said while attempting to soothe her fears, it was enough that they acknowledged them.

Told her they were valid.

"Does that make sense?" Bella asked.

Cassandra had another moment of hesitation, but then it was like somebody inside her snapped their fingers and made everything right again. "Yes," she said. "I think it does." As she got up, she couldn't help but feel Harriet and Bella's eyes upon her. She wondered if they thought she was going to make a break for it, and if they were ready to leap up and rugby tackle her before she got the chance to make it out the door.

As she made her way out of the kitchen and went along the hall, they didn't follow or say anything. When she had stepped over the threshold and brought the front door shut behind her, she knew they weren't going to pursue her. They were leaving the decision up to her.

She was an adult, after all.

Outside, Cassandra took a seat on the front garden wall. She wondered if she was expecting Finn to stroll on by, for him to swoop on down and carry her away in his arms into the sunset as if they had reached the finale of some fifties-era Hollywood film.

In the end, the person who passed by wasn't Finn, but Dorothy.

Cassandra did her best to smile, to put the conversation she had just had with Bella and Harriet out of her mind. "Hi," she said.

"Well, hello." Dorothy was wearing a long jacket which was just short enough to expose his elegant legs, smoothed over by a pair of tights. "Haven't seen you since . . ."

"The dinner with Indigo?"

"The dinner with Indigo."

Cassandra couldn't help but notice the way Dorothy looked up the street, as if impatient to continue. She wanted to tell him he had no need to delay himself here, making conversation. He could keep on his way. But — as always with Dorothy — the opportunity never seemed to come up.

"I notice you ducked out of dancing . . . that you and one of the members of the film crew *mysteriously* disappeared?"

Cassandra felt her face colour slightly. "Was it that obvious?"

"Dearie, it wasn't a fully blown Indigo Miles Midsummer Party. There were few enough people to notice *everything* . . ."

Cassandra went even redder. "Was it rude?"

Dorothy broke out in a grin, and then batted his hand, like a cat clawing at a ball of yarn. "Come on, we're talking about Indigo *Miles* here . . . I'm sure she was delighted to have created the circumstances that allowed such a seedy episode to take place."

Even though this was meant to be a jokey aside, Cassandra couldn't help but feel as if she had done something terribly wrong, or that she had acted uncouthly. As if she and Finn had been all too obvious.

It was more out of a sense for survival than anything else that she threw this back to Dorothy. "You're looking awfully dolled up for an afternoon out in the village."

This time it was Dorothy's turn to blush. "Sometimes it pays off to make an effort." Breaking into a smile, he added, "At least that's what I'm hoping for."

Even though Cassandra wasn't quite sure why, she found herself grinning back. She wondered if it was just because she felt the need to be positive — that she needed to keep herself in a good frame of mind.

"Maybe you'll meet him," Dorothy said, continuing on his way, up the road. "We'll see, shan't we?"

As Cassandra watched Dorothy go, she couldn't help feeling that she had perhaps allowed him to squirm free of the net. That she had failed to put him through the same rigorous probing that he had put her through over Finn.

But, then again, did it really matter?

It wasn't like this was a game of one-upmanship.

Was it?

14

LEAVING TIME

$\mathcal{F}$inn wasn't quite sure what to do with himself. He had packed — and repacked — his bag at least a dozen times. And each time he did so, he made only the most minor of adjustments; changing the position of a sock, or realigning the fold of a shirt, convincing himself there was a bulge in the bag which would cause him discomfort during the short journey out of the hotel and to the van outside. It seemed there was something in the air, because Peter was being just as frivolous with his time. Although his bag had long ago been packed, Peter was spending an inordinate amount of time checking his outfit in the mirror, brushing invisible pieces of lint off the shoulder pads of his jacket.

Constantly jerking his jacket to flatten out non-existent creases in the fabric.

Several times, they had apparently recognised one another for what they were doing, but each time their glances would bounce apart and they would return to their own timewasting. Finally, it was Peter who spoke up.

"Well, I suppose it's time now," he said.

Finn felt a tremble pass through his gut. "Yes, I guess so."

"Everyone will be waiting — down at the van." Peter sauntered over to the window, peered down. "They're all packed up. Standing around. Looking for leadership." He broke into a quick grin as if this was the funniest joke in the world, but the grin disappeared when he met Finn's eye, and they realised they were in a shared predicament.

"You know," Finn said, "I was wondering . . . this village" — the name escaped him momentarily — "*Normonswold*. I think that it has a whole host of stories to tell."

Peter cocked his head to one side. There was a twinkle in his eye — a recognition for what Finn was attempting to do . . . what he was attempting to swing. "Why, I'm glad you said that — very glad. One of us had to recognise it." He broke into an uneasy smile. "It *would* be a waste for us to leave Normonswold with its stories untold, would it not?"

"You don't have anything important planned over the next few weeks?"

Peter pouted. "Goodness, you know as well as I do that we're in the *entertainment* business. What could possibly be so important about *entertainment* that it couldn't be put off . . . at least for a little while?"

Finn felt himself grinning now. "Which one of us should tell them?"

Peter sighed. "I suppose they should hear it from me, since I am the director. I don't imagine they will be all that put out . . ."

It was true that once they had returned the van the film crew would break up, with everyone going their separate ways, working on new projects. It was just the way with the business — all at once brutal, and yet endlessly exciting.

At least Finn always told himself it was *exciting* whenever he felt down about something or other to do with his profession . . .

Feeling in a somewhat roguish mood now, Finn said, "We'll be cutting ourselves off from all outside contact. We won't have our own means of transportation."

"Throwing ourselves at the mercy of the natives."

"Let's just hope they don't prove fierce."

And then the two of them burst into fits of laughter.

It was only about an hour later, when the van had left them behind in Normonswold, and their decision had been made, that Finn wondered just what on *Earth* he was doing.

And then he pictured Cassandra's face in his mind.

And smiled.

15

A COUNTRYSIDE RETREAT

*C*assandra worked away in the studio at Molinaar's Cottage. It was funny how it had just taken a chat with Bella and Harriet to dust away all of the cobwebs from inside her head. It was like it had been years ago, when she hadn't had a care in the world . . . when she had simply been able to *draw*.

She had put away the sketchbook she had taken with her to Pawler's Bay — it had been filed up on the shelf for reference at some future period. She had decided the most important thing for her was she spent serious time with the page, and that she just sketch whatever she found in her heart. And so it surprised her to find that her subconscious was in the mood for work of a slightly darker nature.

Gone were the cutesy couples, or the delicately drawn animals. Now everything she drew seemed to have an edge to it . . .

Before there was always something beautiful about the illustrations — always something *beautiful* — but she found her hand slipping — there was no other way to put it — and adding some wild detail.

An ambiguous glimmer in the eye here.

A curled fist there.

Whenever she allowed Bella to view her work, she couldn't help but survey her as she sat picking through it, wondering if she noticed the subtle changes.

It was a rainy afternoon, with the clouds all bundled up in the skies — damp and wild — when Bella finally thought to pass comment. "There's . . . something," Bella said. "Something to these drawings. Something *different*. Something I haven't seen before."

"Is it bad?"

Bella shook her head immediately, not out of a fear of upsetting Cassandra — Cassandra was sure of this — but out of a sense of knowing her own mind. "No it's nothing to do with the quality of the work. No, that's as good as ever. *Better*, even." Bella continued to stare at the pages. "There's something more . . . *realistic* about these drawings . . . there's more . . . *depth*."

Cassandra felt her chest tighten slightly. "Is that okay?"

" 'Okay' ?" Bella replied, sounding as if she was in something of a daze. "Well, yeah, of course it's *okay* . . ." She smiled again then — turning back to the drawings — the corners of her mouth slackened. "It's sort of a new direction for Humble."

"More dynamic?"

"Yeah," Bella said after a slight pause. Then she slipped Cassandra a sidelong glance. "To be quite honest with you, I feel like I've got my work cut out in finding the words to justify these pictures. But it's a good thing. You're pushing me. We're pushing one another."

"So I'm not sacked?"

Bella sniffed a laugh. "No." She returned to the drawings. "I just hope I'm not going to have to sack myself."

———

Later that afternoon, there was a knock at the door.

Feeling her feet lighter than they had been for months, Cassandra near enough skipped down the hall to answer. When she looked on the person standing there, her breath hitched in her throat. It was Finn.

Every muscle in her body went tense. "Oh, hi," she said.

Finn smiled back at her. He had an umbrella. Raindrops dribbled off it.

Cassandra remembered herself, and — stepping to one side — said, "Please, come in!"

Finn stayed where he was.

Cassandra wondered if he was trying to prove some sort of point.

"Come on!" she said. "You're getting *soaked!*"

"Are you busy at all?"

" 'Busy' ?" Cassandra thought of the dozens and dozens of drawings she had produced that morning. She supposed she *was* busy. And yet she had already done so much. Surely she was due a break? "Uh, no — not really."

"Want to take a walk in the woods?"

A smile snaked across her mouth. "It's tipping it down."

Finn shrugged. "I'm already soaked through — I'm not getting any wetter."

"No, don't be silly. Come in and I'll make you some tea." She thought for a moment, and then added, "Some lunch?"

"I'd much rather get some fresh air."

She held her ground, unsure quite how to react. She supposed part of it was due to all those warnings her mother had given her in her youth — about not 'catching her death' in the rain.

"I . . . do you want to drive?" she asked.

"No car."

"And I don't drive." She glanced over her shoulder, half expecting Bella to be standing there, perhaps wagging an admonishing finger — waiting for her to return to the studio and her work. Cassandra reminded herself they were partners.

Neither of them was the boss.

Cassandra was free.

She could make her mind up on her own.

Make her own decisions.

Like a Big Girl.

Perhaps it was foolishness — maybe it was just a case of being rendered hypnotised by Finn — but she reached for her raincoat, hanging from one of the hooks, tugging it down and shrugging it on over her shoulders.

Even as she stepped outside, feeling the first chilly dampness of the rain at her neck, she felt a kind of childlike delight.

What *would* her mother have said about this?

Since Finn clearly had no idea of where to go or what to do, Cassandra found herself taking the lead. She had surmised that Finn was looking to her for a suggestion of some sort of adventure, and the closest Normonswold came to any sort of adventure at all was the woods, a little way outside of the village.

Once Cassandra got over the dampness, and the cold — cuddling up to Finn, and feeling his strong arm about her helped greatly with this — she allowed herself to slip into the scenery. To become one with the slate greys, and the steely blues.

Water glistened off every surface, raindrops clinging to the foliage.

It dripped down from above; in other places running in torrents.

She had never understood people who complained wholeheartedly about 'bad' weather. She had always enjoyed contrasts. If nothing else, it provided her with inspiration — *more raw materials* — for her artwork. Each and every new experience was a gift to her subconscious. And that was a wonderful thing because she never quite knew whenever some experience would come out in her work. There was a certain randomness about self-expression which never ceased to surprise and amaze her.

She wondered if Finn felt that way about his work.

She might've liked to ask him, but she didn't want to break the soundscape:

The peace and quiet.

The falling rain.

They were right in the middle of the woods when Finn turned into her and said, "I'm willing to admit I was more than a touch foolhardy in suggesting this outing — and in this weather — but are we almost at the end of the walk now?"

She looked out ahead, to the soppy, muddy path before them. She had only been walking in the woods a handful of times herself. "I think . . . there's some shelter just up ahead here?"

Even as she said it, she wondered if she hadn't taken them the wrong way. From all of her walks in the woods previously, it had seemed like a simple route. But the fact she was the one doing the guiding — coupled with the adverse weather conditions — meant the way wasn't as clear-cut, as simple as it had previously seemed.

And so she was deeply relieved that the cabin came into view when they turned the corner.

"Hello?" Finn said. "What's this, then? A cosy little hideout in the woods?"

He squeezed her to his side and a warmth glowed through her blood — she too was anxious to get in the warm and dry, if only for a few minutes, before trudging the sopping-wet path back to the village.

She took the lead, treading on the front step, with Finn falling away slightly.

"Are you sure it's okay?" he asked. "I mean, perhaps this belongs to somebody?"

She felt a thrill pass through her. "Please don't tell me the fearsome Finn Hallchurch, Conqueror of Six Continents, is having second thoughts about breaking into a cabin at the backend of some dank British woods?"

Finn coloured a little at this slight, or perhaps his cheeks were rosy from the weather. Cassandra was willing to give him the benefit of the doubt.

Beginning to feel foolhardy in Finn's company — as if she could do anything at all without consequence — she reached out for the door handle and turned it. Straightaway, she felt it was the right decision.

Warmth wafted over her.

She breathed in the familiar, welcoming scent of wood.

That grassy, syrupy odour of tree sap.

When she brought the door shut behind them, she noticed a dim light in the corner of the cabin. There was somebody lying on top of the camp bed.

They stirred.

16

RUDE AWAKENING

assandra's heart leaped up to her mouth. She felt the blood swill in her veins. She could hear her pulse beating hard against her temple and wondered if the sensation wasn't going to transform itself into something more malicious, like a headache.

She soon got enough of a hold on herself to see the scene clearly — to see the person in the camp bed. It was a boy. He had a handsome dusty complexion. His eyes were dark, and the shape of walnuts. As he sat up against the headboard, he appeared just as surprised at their presence here as they were about his.

Finally, Cassandra found the strength to speak. "Sorry . . . we didn't mean to intrude. We didn't think that . . . well, there was anybody here . . . are you . . . uh . . . are you here all alone?"

It was then more malicious possibilities played out in her mind.

That this person could be some sort of a runaway — a criminal?

The boy looked from Cassandra to Finn, and then back again.

His gaze was penetrating. Profound. When he spoke, he had a slight Indian accent. "I always wanted to stay here. Because this was the place my father loved."

Cassandra thought about the last year — about how Kareema Ashburton had lived out her last moments in this cabin. How many more would this place claim?

"Who was your father?" Finn asked.

"Swapan Drupada."

Cassandra felt her chest tighten. She looked to Finn, as if this would mean anything to him. She shifted her attention back onto the boy. "His name is on the plaque outside . . . he . . ." What Cassandra had been on the cusp of saying was that Swapan Drupada had been Dorothy's lover, and that this cabin was a kind of mausoleum, kept in a pristine state in dedication to his memory.

But she held back for the time being.

The boy shuffled about in bed, propping himself up straighter. He yawned then stretched, glancing out the window. He appeared to gauge the weather outside — the rain sheeting down. "I am Nameeth. I came here on invitation. It was Kieran Doores . . . *Dorothy* . . . who invited me here, to Normonswold."

Cassandra supposed Nameeth to be a few years older than she had first given him credit for. He was probably in his early twenties, rather than his mid-to-late teens. Under their watchful gaze, he shifted onto his feet, setting the camp bed springs creaking. He stared out of the window some more.

"This place is perfect, isn't it?"

Cassandra said nothing. Neither did Finn.

"I mean, it is a refuge away from everything else — somewhere a person can come to escape."

"Yes . . . it certainly is," Cassandra replied.

"How long have you been here?" Finn asked.

"About a week," Nameeth replied, then nodded to the kitchenette. "Dorothy brings me food every day. He asks if there is anything I need. We don't speak much. I think it is painful for both of us . . . we both loved my father." He brightened. "Would you like a cup of tea?"

Cassandra wasn't going to say no, and neither was Finn.

Dorothy kept Nameeth sufficiently stocked up that he had fresh milk to offer, along with a range of fruits and biscuits. In the end, Cassandra went for a bunch of grapes and a buttered scone. She supposed the walk in the adverse weather had stoked her appetite. Nameeth went for a chocolate muffin to accompany his cup of tea. While Finn — apparently considering his figure — held back from partaking in the treats at first, he soon found it impossible to resist one of the macaroons on offer.

The three of them sat in silence, supping tea.

In the end, Cassandra spoke. "How long are you planning to stay here, Nameeth?"

He shrugged. "I don't know. Dorothy said I could stay here as long as I want. As long as I need." He sipped at his tea then set it down on the floorboards. "I won't stay here forever, if that's what you mean. Normonswold is not my place. But it is good to be away from everything. To be away from my problems. To have some time to think things through."

Cassandra felt a pang in her stomach. Something was so familiar about what Nameeth said. It felt as if her whole body was gradually sinking. "I like to be by myself sometimes, too," she found herself saying. "Sometimes it's the best way to figure out what you want."

Nameeth looked profoundly into her eyes. His expression was serious — there was none of the joviality from before.

"Actually," she continued, "I went somewhere to be alone just a week or so ago."

"And she came back with me," Finn put in.

Cassandra smiled, and when she turned back to Nameeth she saw he was smiling too. "You two look very happy together," Nameeth said. "I wish you joy in your union."

Cassandra felt herself flush. When she cooked up the courage to slip Finn a side-long glance, she saw he had gone a shade of red too.

Realising the silence — if not the embarrassment — which hung over the cabin, Nameeth said, "Oh, I'm sorry . . . I just presumed. It was an assumption."

Cassandra held up her hand, her cheeks still feeling warm. "No, really, it's fine," she said, through a smile. "It was just a chance meeting while I was away from Normonswold for a few days. While I was working things out."

"And did you work them out in the end?"

She thought about her increased productivity. About how her stress symptoms had dissolved . . . but had it really been the simple fact of going away for a few days, or had the discussion she had had with Bella had some bearing? She could still recall how she had attempted to run away when she had returned. And how Harriet and George had been called into action to drag her back to Molinaar's Cottage. But in this moment — *right now* — she felt fine about everything. She felt at peace with her work. And she certainly had no complaints about the company she was keeping.

"Yes," she replied finally.

Nameeth grinned. "I am glad to hear it — I hope I will have the same degree of luck. I only ask you one favour when you do leave here — not that you have overstayed your welcome by any means.

Please stay as long as you like. Until the weather has cleared up. *Longer.*"

"What's the favour?" Cassandra asked.

"That you say nothing about my being here. Nothing to anyone in the village. Nothing to Dorothy, either. He wishes my presence here to remain a secret. And we must respect the bond he and my father shared. This is a very personal place for him."

"A refuge, like you said," Cassandra put in.

"A 'refuge' . . . and refuges are to be respected."

"I won't say anything to anyone," Finn replied. "I promise."

"Me neither," Cassandra said. "The last thing I would want if I'd gone away alone to work things out was for two strangers to intrude." She broke into a smile. "And, believe me, I understand the irony of me saying that right now."

Nameeth smiled back. "Thank you. I really appreciate this."

They stayed with Nameeth — chatting and having more tea — until the rain let off, becoming nothing more than a hazy drizzle.

Cassandra and Finn set out from the cabin. As they trod their way up the dirt track, toward the lake around the back of the cabin, Cassandra reached for Finn's hand.

Their fingers entwined.

They walked close together along the path, the treetops towering above, the dimming, steely sky peeping through the gaps. They didn't speak, as if Nameeth's promise already bound them. As if they were already back in Normonswold and had to pretend that they hadn't run into anybody at all while they had been in the woods; and certainly not when they had gone to visit the cabin.

"You know," Finn said, once they had taken a few steps out of the trees, hastily leaving the woods behind. They still walked hand in hand. "Sometimes I wonder if I've spent my whole life trying to be alone so I can work things out." He stared at the path ahead.

"And I can't say that it has ever done any good." He stopped, bringing the two of them to a halt. He looked into Cassandra's eyes, and she looked into his. "Perhaps it's time I found someone else to help me work out what I want — what I *really* want."

She held still. Then she felt a humming in her chest. A slight warmth flowed about her blood, despite the thorough freezing the two of them had been treated to that day. "I already know what I want." She lurched into him, taking him by surprise.

Kissing him violently.

17

A TRUE NORMONSLANDER

*O*ver the course of the next week, Finn spent a lot of time wandering about Normonswold aimlessly. It couldn't have been a simple act of fate that each time he ended up back at Molinaar's Cottage:

Headquarters of Humble Greetings.

But — more importantly — Cassandra's home.

He didn't knock on the door each time he turned up, knowing better than to be so rude as to intrude upon Cassandra while she was busy at work, but he did always linger so someone might come out and ask him inside for a cup of tea.

He supposed under normal circumstances, it would've weighed heavy on his heart each and every time he returned to the Thicket Arms Inn. He had stayed in his share of places run by country bumpkins, but Frieda Smyth really did have a charm which was all her own. And which Finn wasn't all that anxious to scale the depths of.

One thing which made their stay at the Thicket Arms bearable was that — now the film crew had skipped town — they had the place to themselves so Finn and Peter had their own bedrooms. This — coupled with the fact the two of them were now 'between projects' — also presented the upshot that Finn and Peter hardly ever saw one another. It was only on the chance occasion of one or the other of them skulking in through reception — attempting not to disturb Frieda Smyth where she watched television in the back room — while the other was attempting to skulk out, that they had any reason to interact at all. It was as much of an open-secret throughout Normonswold that Peter was romancing Indigo Miles, as it was that Finn was romancing Cassandra.

Secrets didn't stay secret long in this village.

As Finn went on his walks through Normonswold each day, he actively sought out projects he could create for himself. Reasons that would cement himself in Normonswold for at least a little longer. One day, he found himself caught up with the village chapel, and he scoped out the grounds, taking great pains to inspect each and every gravestone, scouring his memory for a spark the names might illicit. But none of the names brought any recollection to mind. He supposed Peter might've had better luck, being better read — more *interested* — in British history and ancestry.

Later, Finn turned his attention to the obvious idea of Ebben-devor, but he soon averted his attention from the place — before he had even set foot on the driveway — recalling that he had heard Peter slipping out of the hotel that morning to go and pay a visit to Indigo Miles. No, it was as if some sort of all-present force was actively attempting to repel him from Normonswold . . . or at least not-so-subtly hinting that there was no professional reason for him to stay.

In his frustration, he retired to the Thicket Arms pub to drown his sorrows with a solitary pint. He was glad to find there was a collection of picnic tables arranged on the grass at the front and he took his place there, supping his beer, getting his thoughts together. He hadn't been sitting there for more than five minutes when he heard a car engine humming along the road behind him.

Soon enough, the sound caught his full attention.

The engine made a deafening *roar* and a thick cloud of fumes wafted through the air. When he turned to look, he saw a large, four-wheel-drive vehicle, with tinted windows, winding its way along the countryside lane. It put Finn in mind of an elephant walking on eggshells — hoping in vain not to crush the delicate objects beneath its feet.

Finn surveyed the vehicle's advance through the village, for the first time realising he had somehow managed to inhabit the gossipy mentality of Normonswold. Now he felt a kind of sympathy for the window-twitchers who kept an eye on every-thing — and from whom came all the news of arrivals and depar-tures. Feeling curious, Finn finished up his pint, leaving the glass on the bench — much to the malign of Frieda Smyth, he was sure — and set off after the car.

It wasn't difficult to keep the car in sight. No car could go much more than ten miles an hour through Normonswold if it didn't want to end up smashing into the side of someone's home, or else drowning in the marshy pond. He caught up with the car before it reached the end of the village. He watched it make its way to Ebbendevor.

Feeling as though he had come to the end of the line — he wouldn't be able to pursue it along the road leading to Ebbendevor — he resolved to return to the Thicket Arms, and perhaps to order another beer, assuming Frieda Smyth hadn't already blacklisted him for the crime of not returning his empty glass to the bar.

As he turned back, he heard the engine again. He realised the car was returning. Perhaps the person had intended to visit Ebbendevor, but — finding the gates locked — had turned around.

The car drew up alongside him.

Finn had all sorts of flashbacks to various movies — some of which he had had a behind-the-camera role in — where government agents would trundle up to some unsuspecting victim in the middle of the street and hustle them inside. This time, though, the car window simply rolled down.

"Excuse me?"

Finn turned to look. He saw a woman of about sixty behind the wheel. She had puffy cheeks and a pressed-on smile. Although Finn wasn't a fan of his ability to jump to conclusions about people, he couldn't help but dislike her immediately.

"Do you know the way to the Knightly Resort and Leisure Complex?"

Finn was rendered stunned for several moments. Then he snapped back to reality. "I can't say I do — or that I was aware such a place existed. At least not around here."

"Well, I wouldn't expect you to know of the place, since it was never built. But you must know the designated site?"

"Afraid not."

The woman pouted, then glanced into the back seat, impossible to see from where Finn was standing. When she turned her attention back to Finn, she was smiling slightly. "What's your name?"

"Finn. Finn Hallchurch."

"You don't have the look of a Normonswoldian to me."

Finn felt a smile sneak across his lips. "What gave me away?"

"Oh, you just have the air of a visitor."

It was strange he should find this remark so cutting — the word 'visitor' was like a knife twisting in his gut.

"No offence intended," the woman continued. She gave a sigh. "You wouldn't be interested in joining our wild goose chase, would you? It might be a nice outing for a tourist."

Again, Finn wasn't all that pleased with being referred to as a 'tourist', although when he got down to it, he supposed that was exactly what he was. What else was he *really* doing in Normonswold?

"Actually," he said. "I'm a filmmaker."

The woman's lips parted but no sound emerged. She fixed her gaze upon him, tilting her head to one side. "You don't say?" A smile crept across her lips. "Well, then, you simply must come along for a quick ride."

"All right," he replied.

The passenger-side door opened and he got in. When he glanced into the back, he saw another woman. She was about the same age as the driver and — Finn noted after a good few brain-scratching moments — an exact replica.

Twins.

The woman in the back seat was working away on a laptop, tapping at the keyboard, doing Finn didn't know what.

As he turned his attention back front and centre, staring out through the windscreen and to the village ahead, he couldn't help but bring to mind that he had somehow found himself behind the wheel of a steamroller.

Ready to crush everything in its path.

18

A WONDERFUL YEAR

*C*assandra woke with a greater feeling of positivity — of well-being — than she had ever previously experienced. It seemed as if her whole body was humming with some strange, undiscovered substance. She had inexhaustible stores of energy.

Once she had bounced in and out of the shower, and thrown on some clothes, she set about making breakfast for everyone. When Bella and Robert — bleary-eyed, though fully washed and dressed — stepped into the kitchen, they were delighted to see the spread which Cassandra had laid on for them.

The fresh coffee.

And the fried eggs.

And the bowls of cereal.

Then — again — their attention returned to the fresh coffee.

Cassandra wasted no time in serving them.

"Happy anniversary!" she declared, opening up her arms to Bella.

Bella shrugged off her lethargy — or whatever it was which

was eating her that particular morning — and fell into Cassandra's embrace. For a few seconds, Cassandra forgot Robert was even there. And then realising he had had just as fundamental a role in Humble Greetings, she gave him a hug also.

"Doesn't seem like it's been a year, does it?" Robert said, flushing slightly as he took his seat at the table.

"Oh, I don't know," Bella said, descending into her own chair, black circles around her eyes, but smiling widely.

Soon after, there was a knock at the door.

Harriet and George appeared there.

"Congratulations!" Harriet said, almost screaming as she threw herself over the doorstep and into Cassandra's arms. When she backed up, her eyes were slightly damp. "Thank you for everything — for making this possible!"

Feeling more than a little embarrassed by this outpouring, Cassandra averted her gaze, focusing on Woss, who had appeared at their shins, tail wagging.

Once they had made a fuss of Woss, they all sat at the table to enjoy the breakfast Cassandra had prepared.

As they sat eating, they shared stories of the past year. All that had happened with Lord Charles, and how it had meant Robert's arrival — and how this had led to the business exploding.

And then there had been George who had returned to the village a year later, when they had been ready to expand. His arrival had helped deliver everything they could've hoped for — bringing them into touch with Kareema Ashburton; and then Sylvia, who had taken over Kareema's assets after her death.

There was no denying Humble was in a truly commanding position, and although Robert was never of the mind to pronounce any start-up a 'success', he had taken to thinking about mid-to-long-term plans, which she took to be a positive thing.

Once they were finished with breakfast, there was a sort of lull as they sat around in comfortable conversation. They started to talk about their favourite greetings card designs. This was a conversation reserved more for Robert, George and Harriet than for Bella and Cassandra, who — *Cassandra at least* — felt somewhat squeamish expressing any sort of opinion about her work lest she ruin it for someone else.

The clock had hardly struck ten when there was another knock on the door.

Indigo Miles appeared, beaming widely, congratulating the whole team on another year of 'rip-roaring' success. Once she had got this particular observation out of the way, she turned her mind to the far more important matter of getting to grips with the party preparations for that evening. The fact there was a party at all, took Cassandra somewhat by surprise. Although there had been a few jokey suggestions they should have a huge celebration at Molinaar's Cottage — she believed the phrase 'garden party' had been thrown around — she had missed the conversation where any sort of plan had been set in stone.

Cassandra's opinion hadn't been factored in.

She was at a loss as to what to do. She soon found the studio had been commandeered as an integral piece of party real estate, and so was exiled to the upper rooms. She attempted to draw, putting down some more ideas, but was distracted by the noise of moving furniture —the grunts and peals of laughter — from downstairs.

She gave up on getting any work done and went downstairs to join the others.

Although she never would've believed it herself, she found party planning actually *enjoyable*. She had always liked to experience Bella's mother Indigo in small doses, but there was no denying that she was great company . . . that she livened up every second that she was present.

Around midday, there was another knock at the door, and Peter — coupled with Dorothy and Harriet's Aunt Adiema — walked in.

The amount of work Indigo Miles had already done was astonishing. The cottage was unrecognisable. Everything was covered with a kind of white cloth — could it be *silk*? Indigo had arranged glass tea lights around the cottage, to be lit later on.

The new-arrivals instantly looked for some way they could make themselves useful, and Indigo wasted no time issuing orders.

Cassandra felt a mixture of disappointment and relief that Finn hadn't arrived with the others. She so wanted to see his face — to be *near* him — and yet, he affected her so greatly — stealing the breath from her lungs — that she was glad he hadn't tagged along with the advance group. She consoled herself with the fact that he would be along later that evening. She was certain Indigo Miles would've issued him an invitation.

Cassandra found herself floating from room to room of Molinaar's Cottage, searching for her role in the preparations. In the end, she was glad when Bella hooked her arm through hers and guided her upstairs, away from the mania.

"We've got business to attend to," Bella said.

Bella went to work in her bedroom, flipping through outfits in the wardrobe as Cassandra perched on the edge of the bed. She couldn't help but notice there was little — if any — space for Robert to keep his clothes in the bedroom. Although Cassandra really didn't think it her place to ask, Bella read her mind.

"Oh, he has some drawers in the spare room — you know how it is for men . . . a couple of suits, underwear, a pair of jeans . . . not complicated."

Cassandra smiled. "Men are lucky."

Cassandra felt trapped in a kind of wind tunnel as Bella tore items of clothing out of her wardrobe and set them upon the bed. She dizzily took stock of the various options. Of the floaty summer dresses. The more sedate, closer-fitting ones which came down to just above the knee.

Bella ordered Cassandra to try each dress on in turn.

And Cassandra did as she was told.

Cassandra thought she was going to get at least a small say in what she was going to wear, but it soon transpired that Bella had no intention whatsoever for Cassandra to express an opinion about anything. She watched on with a hawkish expression as Cassandra pulled on dresses, pouting and shaking her head in turn. When they had got through a good three-quarters of Bella's wardrobe, Cassandra began to despair.

They had certainly left it late to skip out and buy something.

All the shops would be shut by now.

Cassandra thought about how Molinaar's Cottage had been a dress shop in another life — before Bella had acquired the place. They could certainly have done with some of the stock to prowl through.

In the end, the dress came out of nowhere. There were only two left in the wardrobe besides the one Cassandra was currently trying on. As Bella brought it down, Cassandra became bogged in lethargy. She had the helpless sense this dress would be like the others she had tried. That it would be deemed either 'wrong' or 'inappropriate'.

So it was with great surprise that, as she examined herself in the long mirror which hung on the bedroom wall, Bella — flanking her shoulder — did not dismiss the outfit right away. Instead, cocking her head to one side, she frowned, and said, "Well, I think it might be okay if we find some shoes to go with it."

On another occasion, Cassandra might've been left slightly offended by Bella's lack of enthusiasm. But, to tell the truth, she was so worn down by the whole experience of trying out the entirety of Bella's wardrobe that she was relieved above all else. And it seemed a minor miracle when Bella fished out a pair of shoes and pronounced them 'not completely terrible' when combined with the dress.

The dress in question was a burgundy shade. The shoes were a pair of high heels of a slightly lighter colour. Despite the fact Cassandra tottered about on them, attempting to find her balance, they seemed to be fairly agreeable. Since she was more used to getting about in pairs of battered trainers, she supposed anything would seem strange by comparison. More resigned than pleased with her afternoon's work, Bella gave Cassandra a reluctant nod of approval, dismissing her from the bedroom.

Hearing the various noises of exertion from downstairs, Cassandra slipped out of her high heels and tiptoed across the landing to her own bedroom.

Once inside, she set her mind to the process of scrubbing up a bit for the party.

Even though Cassandra took about three times longer than normal to get herself ready, there were still sounds of industry when she ventured down the steps.

She felt as if she was playing a part in a film as she trod down the staircase barefooted, heels dangling from her fingers. She was glad to find everybody was so maniacally fixed on their tasks that she wasn't the centre of attention. It also meant she had a chance to take stock of the preparations Indigo had put into place.

Bunting — if that was the right word for it — hung down from the ceilings. Meanwhile, it seemed as if all of the furniture had been rearranged depending on Indigo's whim. Indigo had certainly taken advantage of having George, Robert, Dorothy and Peter to order about the place — to do all of the heavy-lifting.

Cassandra had a slight moment of panic when she stepped into the studio and saw everything had also been transformed. That the space had been temporarily made available for party invitees complete with chairs and a couple of tables, tea lights everywhere. But she was relieved to find that her sketchbooks, and her works in progress for Humble, had been safely placed in one of the storage cabinets. Because she was paranoid about something — *anything* — happening at the party, she twisted the key in the cabinet lock, and then hid the key under her pillow, in her bedroom. It wasn't so much the fear of the work she had done getting ruined by a spilled drink, or something more malicious. It was more that she hated to show off work in progress.

She wanted to keep her work to herself for as long as possible.

Only at the last moment would she allow the world in.

Almost an afterthought.

When she emerged from the studio and passed Indigo in the corridor, she expected to be issued orders. Indigo, however, merely smiled at her, and — eyes gleaming — pronounced that she looked 'wonderful'.

There wasn't much time for Cassandra to fully appreciate Indigo's assessment because someone was knocking at the front door.

And Cassandra — realising it was still too early for guests to arrive — felt her heart skip up to her throat.

She knew who it would be.

And, even so, when she arrived in the front hall, and when she pulled the door open, a ripple of surprise cast through her.

Tonight he was wearing a suit — unrumpled, and *clean*. He had on a simple white shirt underneath. And a pair of well-polished shoes.

Finn.

19

CELEBRATION TIME

*A*s the party took hold of Molinaar's Cottage, Cassandra did her best to remain grounded. She had to make a true effort to stop her concentration from slipping. If she didn't make a constant effort, her gaze would skip onto Finn, standing beside her. This was problematic because she was supposed to be meeting and greeting all of the guests as they strolled in through the door. She was taken off-guard, slightly, by the formal clothes everybody was wearing. She supposed this was the dress code Indigo had expressed in the invitations which Cassandra had never had the chance to see.

Although the faces were familiar, Cassandra could've done with some prompting for the names from Robert, George or Harriet since she had few dealings with the business side of things. All the same, it didn't appear they expected much from her . . . just the chance to shake her hand and tell her that her artwork was 'simply stunning', or words to that effect.

Even despite the fact that she told herself the only thing which really mattered was that *she* was satisfied with a piece of work before letting it go, she couldn't help but bask a little in the glow of these gushing comments. She told herself it was good for her to get positive feedback . . . at least once in a while.

As long as it didn't go to her head.

Once the party was fully in swing, the benefit of having Finn nearby soon paid off. When ambushed by Indigo Miles and Peter, wishing to know all about Cassandra's 'process' — from start to finish in elaborate detail — Finn stepped in after a couple of awkward minutes, leaping into a hilarious tale about a documentary he had once shot at sea. She allowed herself to be caught up in the story, and to be swept along to its end, until such a time that Finn — *somehow* — had them excusing themselves from the grinning couple. And she couldn't help noticing how Peter's hand had made itself comfortable on Indigo's hip.

She felt Finn's hand flat against her spine. It sent tingles through her bones. It made her stomach sink into the ground.

"Was that okay?" Finn asked. "I'm sorry if I overstepped . . . it's just . . . I thought you looked . . . I dunno . . . uncomfort—"

Before he could finish, she launched herself at him, pressing her lips against his. She felt his whole body seize up — his muscles go tight — as he accepted her kiss. They were in the corridor, where people were casually treading through on their way to viewing the display which'd been put up in the studio to mark Humble's progress. She gently moved Finn around so they were no longer blocking the path . . . so that what they were doing was no longer one-hundred-percent exhibitionist.

Beneath the staircase, and half-hidden from view, they kissed tenderly.

She was glad that — even despite getting himself dressed up for the occasion — Finn hadn't put any sort of product in his hair. She enjoyed combing her fingers through each and every strand, feeling them tickle her palm.

When they finally broke apart, she looked about, half expecting a crowd to have assembled, as if they were some sort of a performance art piece to be scrutinised.

But they were alone.

She surreptitiously led Finn up the stairs — away from the party. The only one who set eyes upon them was Woss, as he trudged away from the joviality, no doubt searching for somewhere quiet to lie down and get some rest.

He trusted that all these people would be gone in a matter of hours.

Cassandra brought her bedroom door shut behind her.

She had no idea what she was doing . . . not in the *middle* of this party.

Anybody could walk in any moment.

And yet, it was impossible for her to resist . . . she *mustn't* resist.

Finn held back, as if she might not quite be in her right mind.

But she was insistent.

She reached up for his suit jacket, quickly and casually slipping it down his arms, allowing it to drop into a crumpled heap. Next, she worked at his shirt buttons, undoing each one in order.

He stared at her with wide eyes.

She pressed her palm flat against Finn's chest. She could feel his heart beating. The gentle rhythm of his pulse . . . growing quicker by the second. He was trembling slightly, but then so was she. When he reached up for the material which tied her dress around the back of her neck, she felt her whole body give a quiver. She drew a sharp breath — all that she could manage.

Her dress pooled at their feet.

Bella had suggested she wear no underwear this evening.

And this — like Bella's other suggestions — Cassandra had taken on board.

They stared into one another's eyes for the longest time. There was a burst of laughter from downstairs. It felt like an invisible audience.

Lightning danced through her veins.

She took hold of Finn.

Led him over to her bed.

She laid him down.

And climbed on top.

THINKING TIME

*A*s Finn stood in the middle of the field — a few miles out from Normonswold — he felt a gentle gust blow across the long grasses. It was chilly, reflecting the mental image of what the slate-grey sky above suggested. He drew his long jacket tighter around him, and thought about how many adventures this particular garment had been through with him. It was funny how he had reached the point of solitude whereby he had begun to think of his clothes themselves as being companions.

Was he closer to losing his mind than he had previously appreciated?

They were late — the sisters — he had agreed to meet them here at midday, on the dot. That punctuality had been their insistence, rather than his own. Although Finn had spent a great portion of his life abroad — losing himself in 'savage' domains — he had never lost the manners instilled in him by his British upbringing. As was his wont, he had got here at about ten minutes before twelve, and now it was ten *past* twelve, he felt an itch of irritation. He thought about how he had had to walk out of town to get here — the rest of the film crew had taken the van back with them, leaving him and Peter without a vehicle. And then he reminded himself just how magical that walk had been . . . the wildlife he had seen, and how it had been wonderful to absorb the landscape of the fields stretching off into the horizon.

He heard the car engine.

He turned on the spot, eyeing the four-wheel-drive vehicle humming its way along. The tinted windows made it impossible to make out those inside. For a moment, a slight panic stoked inside him when he thought it could be absolutely anybody in that car — and that this could all be an elaborate plot to do away with him. Then — for reassurance — he reminded himself that he was in backcountry England, where nothing of consequence ever took place, except perhaps in a mystery novel.

As he awaited the car, he felt his mind spinning back to the party a few nights before — to the time he had spent with Cassandra. He so wanted to return to those moments, to the thrill he had felt to feel her body close to his.

Her skin against his.

Despite the cold weather, he felt a sweat dampen the back of his neck. He turned his mind to other things — to the approaching car.

Finally, it pulled up in front of him.

He breathed in deeply and asked himself just what he was doing.

He reminded himself of who he was . . . a *filmmaker* . . .

The twin sisters got down from the vehicle. They had puffy-cheeked expressions and pressed-on smiles. They also wore identical outfits. Both of them decked out in navy blue trouser suits, with a white blouse underneath. For the occasion, the two of them had tucked their trouser legs into a pair of Wellington boots. Finn thought it was the twin who had been driving the first time he had met them who approached him, although he couldn't be certain.

"Please apologise our tardiness." She inclined her head in the direction of her sister. "We had some makeup issues at Wrought Bar Services."

Finn wasn't quite sure whether or not the woman hadn't simply made up the name of the service station. She could've said anything at all. He was an outsider, and more than willing to take everyone at their word. It took a much greater effort to doubt everything someone said than merely to accept it.

He thought about his previous meeting with the women, and how they had made all sorts of vague suggestions about how Finn could 'tell their story', or 'get across their perspective' with one of his films. And although he was hardly in the business of vanity projects — for his own benefit, or someone else's — there was a sense he should do *something* with his time in Normonswold. The driving factor in agreeing to see the two women again after the brief drive about the village, while having local landmarks pointed out to him, had been that he might at least learn a little more about the surrounding area. That he might improve his local knowledge . . .

"So," the woman continued, turning on the spot. "*This* is our rightful land."

Finn looked about. Fields stretching off in all directions. Apart from the odd tree — here and there — the landscape was featureless.

"This land has been in our family for generations. Our family, you see, used to preside over this region." She pointed off towards a copse of trees, back in the general direction of the village. "Normonswold came into existence so as to serve my ancestors. Without us, there would be nothing."

Finn stretched his mind, looking across the land. Then the obvious thought struck him. He looked the woman in the eye. "If you were such an important family in these parts then wouldn't you have had some sort of a mansion? A country estate?"

"Hah!"

The woman's bark almost made him jump.

"There, Titania, do you see? He is perceptive. *Far* more perceptive than you gave him credit for."

Finn looked over to Titania, unsure just what emotion she might be expressing.

"I am Petunia, by the way," the first woman said.

Finn held himself still. He was certain he had introduced himself, but then again perhaps he hadn't. As he told the two of them his name, he couldn't shake the feeling that they somehow already knew.

"Pleased to make your acquaintance, I am sure," Petunia replied, giving him the slightest shadow of a curtsey. She drew a deep breath, causing her shoulders to sink, and her gaze to shift about. "The bare truth about the country estate — or lack thereof — is that there was something of a criminal rising against my ancestors. In the end, they were driven from their land. From their home. Although stories vary, there are some accounts which proclaim that a great fire brought down the several buildings." She stopped short, as if a director off-stage had caught her eye and given her some silent signal. "You have never heard of our brother, of Lord Charles Knightly?"

Finn shook his head. "No, never."

There was a long silence.

Finn had enough experience of the world to know that he was

missing something big — that he was firmly out of the picture . . . whatever the picture happened to be.

"Well," Petunia continued, "he returned, a year or so ago, wishing to reclaim this land. In truth, it was really a philanthropic gesture — a means of generating some much-needed activity for the flagging local economy."

Finn decided this was a good point to show he wasn't entirely ignorant of local goings-on. "Actually, there is now an internationally renowned greetings cards business in the village. They've been having some stellar success." He stopped, seeing that Petunia was staring razorblades.

"So I have heard." Petunia smiled again. "Still, they don't offer all that much in terms of job opportunities, do they? A *small* operation, if a profitable one?"

Finn couldn't help but think that he had already said too much. So he kept his mouth shut.

"Our brother thought he might be able to beckon the Great and the Good out here with a fine leisure complex . . . however, in the end, he was forced to pull out. The people in the village decided to stand in his way." Here she gave a profound sigh. "A tale as old as the ages. As the ruling class tries to raise standards, the people only wish to pull it all back down into the bog . . . to lower everything to *their* level."

Finn was on the brink of wishing these two unpleasant women goodbye, believing them to be at best disillusioned and at worst dangerous . . .

"Would you like to see what they did?" Petunia asked.

Finn thought through his options.

And decided to play along.

Didn't they say you had to know your enemy?

The twin sisters — the Knightly Twins — led him through a copse and into the field which ran alongside. It was as if he had set foot in an entirely different place altogether.

Gone were the empty fields, sweeping off to the horizon. A whole range of eco lodges sprung up from the earth, everything surrounded by well-landscaped terrain.

The buildings were carefully set into their surroundings — he could tell that due consideration had been taken with the design, so as not to disrupt the natural habitat. Already, he could feel his whole body begin to twitch. His fingers itching to grab hold of a camera and to reel this whole sight in.

There was something about a ghost town which was impossible to get over. There was the silent, macabre majesty of empty buildings. A real sadness that the place would never house human souls. As Petunia led the way, she kept up her unceasing commentary. "You asked about the country estate — about the family home . . . if you were to pull all of this away, and to dig — not too deeply — you would find its foundations. The roots of our family tree."

They continued their progress through the would-be ghost town.

Finn examined how each of the buildings was in perfect condition. He could see no signs of vandalism — only the odd sign of neglect, here and there: flaked-off paint, the chewed-up ends of wooden beams, a cracked windowpane. It was nature, rather than human hands, which had caused the damage.

As they walked, he couldn't help but ask, "Why did you abandon this place?"

"*We* didn't . . . it was our idiot brother."

"I see."

As Titania trailed in their wake, Petunia went on, giving a slight sigh, "He gives in at the first sign of trouble, see? No resilience. No *determination*. Not like the two of us. We never give up."

"So you've come back to rejuvenate this place?"

There was a long silence, and when Finn turned back to look at Petunia, he saw she wore a wide smile smeared across her lips. When she caught his eye, she finally replied, "We're going to tear it down."

MORNING WALK

*C*assandra propped herself up by her bedroom window and peered down into the dainty Normonswold main street. The sun was beaming down. It was soaking up the drizzle which'd fallen the night before, and which soaked the streets. She breathed in the freshness, feeling the warm, clammy sensation gathering at the back of her throat.

The whole world seemed clearer today — she felt as if anything was possible.

She had spent the previous night working on a new collection of drawings, and she had greatly surprised herself by the variety of work which'd emerged from the tip of her pencil. She had laid all the sketches to one side for now. She wouldn't share them with Bella until she was certain they were indeed meant for Humble . . . that happened sometimes — sometimes what came from her pencil lead wasn't to be put on a greetings card at all. The artwork was just all wrong.

When Cassandra got up, she saw it had just gone half past six in the morning. She had a quick breakfast, tossed a few biscuits into Woss's doggy bowl, and then skittered out of the house, wanting to take advantage of the beautiful morning.

Wanting to feel the sunshine on her skin.

As she strolled along the street, she realised just how long ago it seemed that she had attempted to run away from Normonswold. It was such a stupid thing for her to have done. She could never imagine doing something so childish, so idiotic, again . . . although she realised just how easy it was to be wise after the fact.

She had been walking for about an hour — perhaps longer — when she spied Dorothy humming along in his car. He eyed her, waved, and then pulled over.

Unlike on other occasions, Dorothy was wearing a suit. He was on his way to work. Often she wondered why Bella didn't find a role for Dorothy at Humble — she imagined he would relish the prospect of being able to wear a dress to work each and every day.

"Good morning," Dorothy said, rolling down the driver's window.

"Morning."

"You're up awfully early."

"I just woke up like this."

"What a life of luxury and bohemia you lead."

Cassandra couldn't help but grin, because if there was anything remotely 'bohemian' about Humble Greetings, then she failed to see it. They had structure, organisation . . . or, as Robert would have put it, 'a business plan'.

"What're you doing today?" Dorothy asked.

It still felt surreal for Cassandra to be seeing him dressed in a suit, although she knew the reality was he dressed up like this for work.

"What I do every day," Cassandra replied. "Draw."

"Well, you're not drawing right now."

Cassandra smiled back. "I'm composting."

" 'Composting' ? What on *Earth* is that?"

"It's kind of like letting my subconscious get itself sorted out — allowing it to move the furniture about in my brain. Get things in their right place before I shamelessly loot it for all of its ideas."

Dorothy smiled, sighed, then gripped the steering wheel. He shook his head, added, "Bloody bohemians," then trundled off up the road.

As she watched him go, she couldn't help but notice he was heading for the woods. Not the most direct route out of Normonswold. She supposed he was going to see the boy — Nameeth — in the cabin. She wondered how much longer he would stay in the vicinity of Normonswold. She supposed that, really, it was none of her business.

When Cassandra returned to Molinaar's Cottage, she found everyone else gathered around the breakfast table.

Bella, Robert.

George and Harriet.

There was a whole host of breakfast items. Freshly squeezed orange juice. Poached eggs and toast. Steaming cups of hot coffee. Woss was snoozing in the corner, his paws muddy, already having apparently been on his morning walk. Cassandra had expected laughter, a sense of jubilation, so she was taken off guard by the sombre mood.

"Who died?" she asked, immediately regretting her base attempt at humour.

"Take a seat," Bella replied.

Cassandra felt herself begin to tremble. She wondered if she was going to get sacked, or something. Nobody had their eyes upon her. If it had been something personal then they would've been staring holes.

Her muscles all pulled tight.

"It's about my mother," Bella said.

Cassandra's heart beat hard. "Your mother? Is she okay?"

Bella smirked, looking across the table. "Well, that depends on your point of view."

Cassandra examined the others' expressions, seeing what she could decipher from their faces. They gave nothing away, that was for sure.

"We're all rather worried," Bella continued, "about her fraternisations with this director person."

"Peter?" Cassandra put in, and then immediately regretted it when the whole table turned on her.

"That's right," Bella said, with a slight smile. "You were the first one to meet him — what were your impressions?"

Feeling as though she was standing trial — that whatever she said now could easily be used against her in the future — she took effort to measure her words. "Well, he seems like a nice man. From what I've seen of him."

"Anything obvious about him? Any obvious flaws?"

" 'Flaws' ? Like what?"

"You know the ones. Displays of greed, anger, jealousy . . . all of the above?"

"Uh, nothing that stands out."

Bella nodded but didn't take her eyes off her. "It's just that you're the one who brought him here, so I thought you might have a better idea of what he wanted."

"Well, I brought both Finn and Peter here."

"Hmm, and that's what worries me."

Here Cassandra felt herself blush. She didn't really understand why. It wasn't like she was a teenager. She could control herself if she wanted to — if she really put her mind to it she could keep a lid on her emotions.

"Do you think he's after the house?" Cassandra asked.

"He's certainly after something, all right," Bella said, nodding across the table to George and Harriet. "They took Woss out for his morning walk. Into the grounds surrounding Ebbendevor."

"And?"

"*And*, when they got close enough to the house, they happened to see Peter striding his way down the staircase in nothing but a dressing gown."

This statement was met with silence.

Cassandra felt like laughing. But she held herself together. "What do you plan to do about it? It's not like your roles are reversed. She's *your* mother."

Bella bowed her head. "I just don't want to see her getting hurt — not again."

Silence fell upon the table.

With a canine yawn, Woss rose from the floor, where he had been sleeping. He went through the routine of stretching his entire body, working out all of the knots and aches before circling over his bed and lying down once again.

Bella shook her head and said, "Some of us have it easy."

A VIEW FROM THE LAKE

Since it was such a beautiful day, Cassandra decided to go outside to draw. She plucked up everything she thought she needed and headed for the woods.

Birds twittered in the branches. Squirrels scuttled back and forth across the ground, chasing one another. Wild flowers bristled up amongst the long grasses.

She was already halfway to the cabin when she remembered herself.

When she recalled Nameeth was there.

As she approached, she diverted her path, taking the route around the lake so as not to violate his privacy. She eventually came to rest on the other side of the lake, with only a view of the back of the cabin. Although she hardly felt completely comfortable about her position — it would have been the exact place a spy would take up if they were attempting to observe someone in secrecy — she was realistic that it was the best compromise she could make.

She withdrew her sketchbook and lost herself in the scene unfolding before her.

As she drew, she felt the uncollected thoughts skitter through her brain. She thought about how when she had been a child she had believed going outside was boring — that there was nothing to see. It was only when she had reached adulthood that she had realised the precise opposite was true. And that — in truth — it required the power of an adult brain to truly fathom the depth of nature, of the Great Outdoors.

Perhaps that was the explanation . . . that the world outside was simply too overwhelming to be taken in by inferior minds.

That, actually, explained an awful lot about the world.

Half an hour passed by, and then a whole one . . . soon enough, she could feel the warm air beginning to chill. The cool evening breeze beginning to blow. Still, despite the gooseflesh prickling her arms, she had no urge to return to Molinaar's Cottage just yet.

She wanted to be out, among nature, a little longer.

There was something so *inspiring* about being out here.

Something was always happening.

She focused her mind on drawing the scene at the very edge of the lake. A group of guillemots splashing about, bathing their wings, glugging back water with their beaks, their delicate throats throbbing as they did so.

Birds had always been a difficult prospect for Cassandra. There was something about their shape which was difficult to fully capture on a piece of paper. Or maybe it was just the way they moved. The fact that they flew. It just seemed to be so marvellous — so *make-believe*. But she did her best, flipping the pages of her sketchpad as she went about her work, furiously scratching away.

It was only when she sensed motion out of the corner of her eye that she came to a halt. She looked off in the direction of the cabin — the source of the movement. She allowed her sketchpad to dip slightly in her hands. She squeezed it between her thighs.

Dorothy.

He was still dressed in his suit.

Coming along the path, towards the cabin.

She held still, feeling she was intruding just to be sitting where she was. She wondered if she should slip away . . . if she should disappear into the trees.

But she remained.

Dorothy closed on the cabin. His whole attention was fixed on the building. If he ever looked up, then she missed it. She knew now was the perfect time for her to get away. That she had long enough to get away from the scene. And yet, she found it impossible to get the message through to the rest of her body.

So she remained where she was.

When Dorothy didn't emerge from the cabin, she brought her sketchpad up and continued to draw whatever came to mind. It was difficult to get her hand limber — to channel into her subconscious and express the ideas held there. She was distracted. She knew the sensation well. And she knew she should just get over herself.

But she couldn't.

About ten minutes later — and with nothing of any particular substance committed to her sketchbook — she caught movement out of the corner of her eye.

A pair of figures emerged.

Dorothy and Nameeth.

Her eyes locked onto the two of them. She remained pinned to the spot. She watched on as Nameeth trudged along with a sports bag slung over his shoulder. The two of them continued on their way — unaware of their observer — heading out of the woods, returning to the car park.

Cassandra remained where she was for another half an hour or so, but found it impossible to return her concentration to her sketchbook.

Soon enough, she gave up.

Right when she was on the brink of slipping her sketchbook away in her bag, and heading back home, a spark of inspiration struck. She slumped back down on the ground, and felt her hand take on a mind of its own — she had barely time to keep up.

Before she knew it, she had sketched out the whole scene, complete with the figures of Dorothy and Nameeth. The two of them with their heads bowed, solemnly traipsing off along the dirt track.

On her way back down, she visited the cabin, went in through the unlocked door to see how everything had been set in its right place; how the floor had been swept; how it looked as if nobody had even ever stayed there at all.

As she set off back through the woods, she supposed Dorothy and Nameeth were already at the train station. Preparing to say their farewells.

Just to think of it made her somewhat sad.

But then she reminded herself she really knew nothing about either person, and that she couldn't project her own emotions onto them.

23

SHARING IS CARING

$\mathcal{C}$assandra spent the next few days working hard at producing as many sketches as she could muster. She allowed them to gather into a pile of papers, determined that Bella would find something of value among what she saw as unworthy cast-offs.

Each time she got through with another sketch, she found herself coming back over and over again to the image of Dorothy and Nameeth making their exit from the woods. She had to force her hand away — several times —from producing the same sketch. It was too personal. That moment hadn't belonged to her.

One afternoon, with the light turning golden, and the sun sinking on the horizon of the warm evening, she was glad to hear the knock at the door disturbing her.

She left behind the sketches and went to answer.

Finn.

"Hi," he said, grinning widely.

Her heart bobbed in her throat. She cast her mind back to the time they had shared at the Humble Greetings anniversary party. She thought about how the two of them had snuck away . . . how they had been together . . . it seemed as if it was a long time ago now. She supposed the two of them had been absorbed in their day-to-day lives; that they had both gone about their own routine.

Romance was like a delicate flame.

It was so easy to extinguish.

She could *feel* how precarious — how *delicate* — it was.

She stood aside, allowing Finn to enter. "You decided to stay a few more days, then?"

"Well, Frieda Smyth makes me feel so welcome at the Thicket that I don't see how I can ever leave."

She suppressed a chuckle then led him into the kitchen. With a practised gesture, she jabbed the kettle on, starting the water boiling. "What have you been doing?"

Finn was sweating slightly and he set about yanking his jumper off over his head.

Cassandra herself was wearing a v-necked shirt over a pair of cut-off jeans.

"You're wrapped up warm," she said.

"You're the one making a cup of tea." He laid his jumper across the back of his chair, puffed out his cheeks, then said, "At this time, it's colder once you get out of the village — out into the country-side a bit."

"I didn't realise you were the nature type. Some documentary?"

He shrugged. "Something like that."

"Something to entertain yourself for a while . . . some way of plying your trade in the middle of nowhere?"

"It's funny the stories you come across in the middle of nowhere."

"Is it?"

He tapped his nose. "It involves twins, that's all I'll say."

"Nothing else?"

"You're an artist, you know how we like to hold our cards close to our chest. Giving things away too soon ruins the surprise."

"So you are making a film?"

"I'm keeping my options open."

She met his eyes and felt same spark pass between the two of them. Then she shook her head and returned to the boiling kettle.

When they were through with their tea an idea struck Cassandra. Even despite the intimacy the two of them had shared, they were both somewhat withdrawn. She knew it was because they hadn't yet spent much time together — they hadn't had much of an opportunity to *really* get to know one another. Not that it meant things were moving too fast . . . she had spent enough of her life waiting.

Deciding it fell to her to push things along, she rose up from the kitchen table. "I'll show you mine if you show me yours."

Finn was rendered stunned for several moments. Then he turned a slight shade of red. "Excuse me?"

Feeling her bravado slip ever so slightly, her voice wavered. "I mean, I'll show you my work-in-progress, if you'll show me yours?"

"I . . . don't really have much to show . . ."

"That's all right, as long as you've got something to tell, I'll let it pass."

Finn closed one eye as if aiming a pistol. "Okey doke. I accept. But on one condition."

"What's that?"

"Secrecy. Not one word to anybody else. And I don't tell anyone about what you show me. Deal?"

She leaned over the table and shook his outstretched hand.

With the preliminaries done with, she led Finn through to the studio, to where she had been scratching away for what felt like days and days on end.

It was only when they crossed the threshold that she realised how big of a deal this was. Throughout her entire life, she had shucked off the idea of showing her works-in-progress to anyone. Already, she was second-guessing herself, wondering whether or not she was making the right decision. The closest she had ever got to doing what she was doing now was in sharing sketches with Bella — allowing her to decide which ones would make good greetings cards.

She was glad Finn held back with a kind of reverential patience. He was waiting for an invitation to look over her work. She was glad they understood one another without speaking. Throughout her life she had been told over and over — by parents, teachers, employers — about how she should 'open up', how she should be more 'outgoing' . . . as if she might achieve those qualities simply by clicking her fingers.

Simply by wishing them into existence.

There was a lot more to communication than mere words.

It'd taken such a very long time for her to truly realise that.

She went through the motions, leafing through the sketches she had produced that day. She handed them over to Finn with a word of apology for each. She noticed how each time she apologised her words became quieter, until she stopped speaking entirely. And then she realised there was *no need* for apologies.

She had asked Finn if he wanted to see her work.

And he had agreed to.

What was more, he would return the favour.

Although she attempted to busy herself shuffling papers around while Finn considered the latest pile of sketches she had laid upon him, she couldn't help but snatch several side-long glances. To try and read the emotions on his face as he considered the latest drawing. She tried to work out what was going through his mind — exactly what emotions her drawings were producing in him.

But it was so difficult.

She had *always* found it difficult to read men . . . if not down-right impossible.

They all seemed so stone-faced.

Seeing that Finn wasn't yet exhausted from looking through her apparently never-ending work, she continued to search the piles of drawings, trying to find something she believed would click with him. In truth, she was just giving him whatever came to hand — hoping she might elicit something . . .

And then he spoke.

"What's that one? Over there?"

Her heart pounded. It was the first thing he had said to her since they had set foot in the studio. She looked to where he pointed — unable to process just what he was getting at. And then the penny dropped. He had picked up the sketch she had done a few days ago, back in the woods. The sketch which depicted Dorothy and Nameeth leaving the cabin. She parted her lips to explain, but Finn beat her to it.

"This is Nameeth and Dorothy, isn't it?"

A numbness set in.

She could only nod.

She expected Finn to insist she put them on a greetings card.

But he said nothing.

He merely smiled at the sketch, and then laid it down.

She gazed at Finn. "I reckon you've seen enough for the time being. Am I right?"

"To be honest, I could sit here with you and look at them all day.

Her heart throbbed against her ribcage. Unsure whether or not he was being fully truthful, she decided to give him the benefit of the doubt. She rose up from where she had been crouched over, replacing the sketches in their place for Bella to look at later.

She exhaled long and hard. "So, what's this top-secret project you're working on?"

Finn averted her eyes. "Like I said, it involves twins."

"Yeah, that's what you told me before."

Finn smiled again. This time he met her eyes before looking up to the ceiling. "Well, we're out in the countryside. They are descended from nobility. And they want me to tell their story." He met her eye again.

She waited for more.

But that was it.

That was all he was going to give her . . .

Feeling as if something was breaking within her, she glared back. She had given everything — she had put it all on the line . . . and he was giving her the absolute minimum in return.

"Sorry," Finn added, lamely. "That's . . . I don't know what else to say . . . I kind of promised to keep things under wraps. At least for now. When I can say more you will be the first to know."

Anger rising in her, she turned back to her sketches. She felt herself beginning to tremble. It was as if she had broken an unspoken promise with herself forged long ago.

And that she had broken it for no good reason.

"Don't worry," she replied. "We all have our secrets." She could feel a prickling sensation around her eyes. She made herself busy with the piles of sketches. "I should get back to work — we can speak later, okay?"

Finn lingered, clearly weighing up his options. But, in the end, he thanked her for the tea, and for showing her the sketches, and then made his exit.

When she heard the front door click shut, she grabbed hold of an empty mug and hurled it against the wall. It shattered into a thousand pieces.

She fell into a nearby armchair, breathless.

Betrayed.

DISCOVERY

*F*inn felt the cool, earthy breeze blowing against his face. The leaves in the trees rustled in the wind. Although the sky was clear and the sun beat down, out here, in the middle of a field, he was exposed to the elements. He clung onto his camera, looking through the view-finder, trying to find his best angle for the current scene.

The twins — Petunia and Titania — were plodding their way across the field, marshalling a team of half a dozen archaeologists, who were carrying all manner of sensory equipment, apparently attempting to divine just what was beneath the surface of the earth. Although Finn could appreciate this was an important step for both the archaeologists and the twins, he found it difficult to become completely enraptured by the process. Even on a beautiful day such as this one, the scene looked very much like a whole group of people bumbling about in a field without much thought or organisation.

In addition, Petunia would often wave for Finn to approach.

For him to bring his camera closer. He did as instructed, following Petunia's orders for him to film this or that thing. He had to admit he was already having reservations about taking on this project. Necessity was the source of all manner of complications. Although he had convinced himself the project was an interesting one — that it had its individual merits — he knew deep down that the only reason he had taken it on was so he would have a logical reason to stick around Normonswold a little longer.

And for what?

He had clearly pissed off Cassandra a couple of days ago when she had set about showing him her sketches. He had no idea what she had been playing at, proposing that she show him her works-in-progress. And yet, when she had asked, he had been unable to resist accepting. He had so wanted to see her work . . . and he had truly thought it would be easy for him to give details about his own work-in-progress — and so return the favour. But, apparently not. There had been some sort of block in his mind.

Something preventing him from fully opening up.

If he was truthful, he could identify the 'something'.

He was so paranoid that someone else's opinion before the right time — before the project was ready — might affect his art in some way. But could he truly even consider this documentary he was making for Petunia and Titania 'art'?

He knew the answer, of course. Anything he did — even if it was 'work-for-hire' — was by definition part of his art. It required the abilities he had forged into his mind over years and years of practice. Whatever he thought personally about the merits of Petunia and Titania's project himself, he lacked the ability to 'switch off' the skilled labour he was investing in it. It was impossible for him to do a shoddy job. Perhaps it was just some expression of pride, or arrogance . . . but that was the truth of the matter.

As day slipped into night, and after he had changed several batteries in his camera, he got the impression the archaeologists were losing heart. He also picked up the signs of stress beginning to show on the faces of the twins. He supposed they didn't have a limitless budget to spend on this horde of archaeologists.

It was just as the sun had dipped behind the horizon, and the moon began to shed its light over the landscape, that one of the archaeologists let out a cry.

As one, everybody moved towards her.

Realising he was down to the very last few minutes of battery, Finn switched his camera to standby. At the back of the excited group — at the front of which stood the twins — he strained to see what was going on.

The archaeologist, down on her knees, was fumbling away with a machine Finn didn't recognise. All he could make out were lines snaking their way across a screen. Several times, she hunched over the laptop sitting to one side, her fingers flurrying across the keyboard, issuing expert instructions.

There was a collective gasp from the archaeologists.

They began to mutter among themselves.

Throughout the course of the afternoon, Finn had been unable to help but pick up on some of the odd conversations between the archaeologists. And he had surmised that — in truth — they were here on pretty much the same pretences that he was.

They were getting paid.

And, like him, they hadn't many expectations about this day bringing forth much more than a much-appreciated lump sum.

However, everything had changed.

There was excitement now.

Feeling part of it — albeit as an outsider, as the man with the camera was always doomed to feel — he tried to capture something of what was going on. As the last scrap of battery drained away, and the viewfinder went dead, Finn leaned into an archaeologist standing beside him and whispered, "What's going on?"

"We think we've found the entrance."

"The entrance to what?"

The archaeologist was rendered distracted for several moments, apparently swept away by the exciting things taking place on the laptop screen. Then he turned back to Finn. "The entrance to the underground railway."

Finn sank back on his heels. He glanced about, feeling somewhat like a spare part now his camera had died. He was only here as a witness now and — to tell the truth — he had little to no idea of what he was actually witnessing.

Once the initial excitement had bubbled down, he managed to squeeze his way through the group to where Petunia and Titania stood. They both gazed down intently at the laptop screen. "Would you mind filling me in?" Finn asked.

Petunia turned to him. "It's exactly what we expected — it confirms all of the family history. A *wonderful* discovery."

Finn remained perplexed. "I thought we were going to make a film about knocking down the leisure resort your brother had built?"

To be fair, Finn's tone was somewhat insensitive, but Petunia seemed to take it with good humour. She laughed then patted him on the shoulder. "All in good time, my dear director. Don't you worry. There will be plenty of 'big money' shots to come!"

Finn felt himself slipping away from the scene slightly. He had to make an effort to stay focused. To stay with them.

Then Petunia said, "Go back to your hotel room and get some rest. You'll want to be here bright and early tomorrow morning when they start up again. I've heard they'll be able to get quite the array of equipment, and at such short notice!"

Petunia's enthusiasm was infectious, and Finn found it impossible not to match her smile as he turned away and headed off through the excitable archaeologists, ready for the solitary walk to the Thicket Arms.

As he walked by himself in the starlight — with the moon lighting his way, and with the stirring of animals in the undergrowth all around him — he thought about how wonderful it would've been to have Cassandra with him. To think, if he had shared just a little more about what his current project was — if he had given back something close to what she had given him — then they could've been together right now.

There was nothing like the realisation that an opportunity had slipped through his fingers. That he had somehow wasted time.

He resolved to put it right.

Cassandra deserved it.

25

SPIES

*C*assandra woke with a start.

She was still dressed in her clothes — a pair of jeans, with a jumper pulled down over her tank top. She was lying on the sofa in the studio.

Outside, she could see it was dark. When she had found her sketching to be coming slowly, she had resolved to have a lie-down. It was incredible what lying on a sofa and closing her eyes could do for her mind . . . it was almost as if it would piece itself back together while she waited. She had used the trick so many times, and had more often than not been rendered surprised at the results as she returned to work refreshed.

This time, though, she had allowed herself to go too far into relaxation and she had fallen asleep. And now it was night-time.

Across the room, a floorboard creaked.

She sat up straight, startled.

Her eyes were still growing accustomed to the darkness. It

appeared to be shifting around her like sooty quicksand. It was impossible to concentrate on any given detail.

But then she made out a shape — a silhouette.

"Cass?"

Cassandra recognised the voice straight away, of course.

Bella.

It was then she noticed another figure alongside Bella.

"You weren't sleeping, were you?"

Harriet.

Her eyes now somewhat used to the gloom, she could tell Bella and Harriet were dressed head to toe in black clothing. This observation confused her for a long moment. Then she made peace with it . . . abnormal things happened all the time around Humble Greetings . . . she supposed the only real surprise was that Woss wasn't lagging at their heels, similarly dressed up.

"Come on, Cass," Bella said.

" 'Come on' where?" she replied, feeling sleepiness tugging at her once more.

"We're going on a secret mission."

She inched onto the edge of the sofa, realising she wasn't going to get her way. She yawned then stretched. "Do I need to put on black clothing, too, or can I go as I am?"

From somewhere, someone — Harriet? — flipped on a lamp.

All of a sudden, the whole studio flooded with light.

Cassandra squinted in the blaze, holding her forearm up to shield her eyes.

"We've already thought of that," Bella said, and Cassandra saw she held a pile of neatly folded black clothing.

Outside, the night-time air was pleasantly warm, although Cassandra could think of about a thousand other things which might've been more pleasurable than prowling through the darkness in a black tracksuit with two of her colleagues. They were making their way out of Normonswold, headed along the road which led up to Ebbendevor.

In the trees, she heard an owl making throaty *woo-woo* sounds, coupled with the *scuttle* of mice through the undergrowth. She supposed — on balance — that she would rather be a woman dressed all in black than a rodent.

Bella led them up to the gates of Ebbendevor. She paused briefly, and then, with practised grace, opened the gate gradually. Cassandra supposed Bella had sneaked into Ebbendevor more times than she could count . . . and that she was an expert at getting into the property without her mother finding out.

She wondered just what Bella needed her and Harriet for.

Once they were out onto the driveway, Bella picked up the pace, threatening to leave Cassandra and Harriet behind. As they went, Bella explained in hurried tones.

"At this time, Mum's usually in the kitchen. But there's a chance — since she has company — that she might be in the living room around front. If she is, and she doesn't have all the lights switched on, or the curtains drawn, she will have a perfect view of the drive."

Cassandra had the urge to suggest to Bella that they not risk being discovered at all — that they simply return to Molinaar's Cottage and forget all this . . .

Whatever it *was* they were doing.

As they crept closer and closer to the house, Cassandra realised increasingly that there was little to no prospect of them turning back.

Before she knew it, Bella and Harriet were standing at one of the back doors. "Okay," Bella said, in a whisper, "we *need* to stay together — and we *need* to be as quiet as we can manage. Is that clear?"

Neither Cassandra or Harriet dared contradict her.

"Good," Bella said, shifting her attention back to the door. She gently turned the handle, frowned as it stopped. Then a sly grin parted her lips. She glanced to Cassandra and Harriet. "This door is *never* locked . . . so there must be something untoward going on."

Cassandra decided not to ask Bella to expand on what this 'something untoward' meant. She watched on helplessly as Bella moved a ceramic turtle to one side to reveal a rusty key. Still grinning, she slipped it into the lock, and turned.

The mechanism clicked.

Bella looked to Cassandra and Harriet. "Be quiet, okay?"

As Bella opened the door and stepped over the threshold, Cassandra had never felt a stronger urge to turn back in her life.

They entered the house through a narrow passageway which Cassandra supposed had served Bella throughout childhood as the perfect secret entrance — or exit.

Cassandra needed to tuck her elbows in so they didn't collide with the walls on either side. She stayed on Harriet's heels as Harriet followed Bella.

Although Cassandra had visited several times, she still didn't know Ebbendevor all that well. She supposed next time she came on an official invitation, she would need to ask for the Grand Tour.

They emerged in an antechamber.

There were various hats and coats hanging from hooks, while there were boots and shoes bundled beneath the benches which ran underneath.

Before Cassandra had the chance to comment, Bella spoke — reading her mind.

"To be fair to Mum, some of this mess is mine," she said, still whispering. "Like in that lot" — she gestured vaguely off to the corner — "there's a couple of shoes and coats which belong to me."

Cassandra stood stock still, overwhelmed by Indigo Mile's wardrobe overspill.

From somewhere in the house, there was a cough.

A dim light blinked on.

All three of them pivoted.

Turned their attention to the semi-circle of the entryway up ahead.

They witnessed Peter — dressed in a shirt and jeans, and a pair of ill-fitting slippers — tread past.

Cassandra and Harriet immediately looked to Bella. Although Cassandra could hardly speak for Harriet, she herself was wondering just what effect actually *seeing* Peter here in her mother's house had on Bella. There was no time for speculation, however, as Bella mouthed, "After him!" and broke into a jog.

Cassandra was unsure at the sudden burst of speed. She felt a smile sneak onto her lips, realising just how childish she felt to be rushing through this house, giving hot pursuit to an unsuspecting man in his sixties. And she couldn't quite shake the idea that he was most likely merely headed off to the bathroom, to take care of business.

Peter continued on his way up a staircase. Once he had slipped from view, Bella gestured for them to follow.

Cassandra found it the most difficult challenge of the night to get up the staircase without causing the floorboards to creak. She did her best to follow Bella's example, but found it difficult to both concentrate on keeping her balance, and focus on treading exactly where Bella had. From what she could hear of Harriet behind her, though, she wasn't doing any better. Cassandra supposed Bella was hedging her bets — no doubt hoping her mother would write off any strange noises to the familiar 'house sounds' which surely accompanied any building of Ebbendevor's age.

At the top of the stairs, it was still dark — it appeared Peter hadn't managed to locate the light switch.

Bella stared at one of the doors — the only one with light leaking out from around the edges. She approached, tiptoeing.

Cassandra was still unsure about Bella's plan . . . was she planning to spook Peter into leaving by pretending to be some phantom while he was in the bathroom?

Soon, though, all became clear.

Bella reached out and slowly turned the doorknob. As she did so, light rushed out of the room and onto the landing — temporarily blinding all three of them.

Within the room, Cassandra immediately saw Indigo Miles, perched on the edge of a pristinely made guest bed. She clutched her hands in her lap in a way which reminded Cassandra of a Catholic schoolgirl attending a church service. She looked at the three of them with wide-eyed alarm. Lips slightly parted.

Cassandra's focus moved onto Peter, who was standing at the bookcase. He, too, had turned to look at them with wide eyes. He was in the process of pulling something out from the bookcase. A photo album?

Indigo Miles found her voice. Even in the moment, Cassandra couldn't help but think it would take much more than a mild fright to silence Indigo Miles. "Just *what* do the three of you think you are doing?"

None of them responded.

Indigo quivered, straightened her shoulders, and then rose to her feet. "Get out of this house — *now!*"

Bella stood her ground. She looked to Peter. It surprised Cassandra just how calmly she responded to her mother . . . Cassandra supposed that she was well-accustomed to managing her mother's melodrama. "What're you doing here?"

"That's absolutely *none* of your business!" Indigo replied.

Bella nodded to the bookcase. "You're showing him the family photographs, aren't you?"

A hardness entered Indigo's glare. "Isabella," Indigo said, "if you do not leave this house at once, I am of a mind to contact the local constabulary."

Cassandra had to resist the urge to chuckle at this remark — knowing that the 'local constabulary' was a solid half an hour's drive away . . . and that they would take a dim view of having to come all the way out here on such pretences:

A woman sneaking into her childhood home, albeit with bizarre motives.

Bella turned her attention onto Peter. "How many of them has she shown you?" Her voice cracked a little. "Has she shown you pictures of my father?"

Peter remained speechless. He met Bella's eye for about half a minute, and then he averted her gaze. It was as good as a 'Yes'.

When Indigo spoke again, her voice was more measured, although her anger was clearly still present. "It is of no consequence to you, Isabella, what I choose to show, or not show, Peter."

"I thought they were *our* secrets," Bella replied.

Indigo said nothing. Then she glanced to Cassandra and Harriet. "The two of you may leave. This is a discussion for myself and my daughter to be having."

Cassandra exchanged glances with Harriet, and the two of them — each with a quick, apologetic look at Bella, turned and fled.

As they made their way down the staircase, treading again through darkness, Cassandra heard Indigo scolding Peter to stay right where he was. As the two of them ventured out of Ebbendevor — this time through the front door; a route familiar to both of them — Cassandra couldn't help but feel a sharp note of sympathy for the man.

He seemed to have got himself caught in quite a *situation* . . .

But, then again, who was Cassandra to judge when it came to romance?

She had got herself into quite a situation herself.

26

APOLOGY

*I*t was overcast and dull at mid-morning when Cassandra looked up from her work and saw Finn striding along the road. The air was infused with the honey-scented incense Cassandra had set burning — it sharpened the dull, damp smell which accompanied the burgeoning clouds.

Finn set such a determined stride that Cassandra began to believe that he was going to carry right on his way, not bothering to so much as glance before passing Molinaar's Cottage. However, right as he was about to slip from view, he did turn.

And marched right up the front path.

When the doorbell rang, Cassandra felt a shudder pass up her spine. She remained where she was — pencil in hand, half-realised sketch in front of her.

She was alone right now.

Since Bella and Robert had gone off to take Woss on a walk that morning, and Harriet and George had gone out for the day to the City, Cassandra was by herself.

Cassandra toyed with the idea of staying where she was. She wondered if she could get away with just pretending she hadn't heard him at all.

But — apparently reading her mind — she saw him take a few steps back along the path leading to the front door and peer right in through the window.

She knew she should've picked out a room around the back of the house to be her studio . . . although none of those rooms had the satisfactory lighting that this one did . . .

Deciding her manners outstripped her sense of fury at their last meeting — how she had bared her soul and he had returned the favour only by clamming up completely — she rose from her desk and trod through the silent house.

She hesitated a few moments at the door, taking deep, cleansing breaths, trying to get some sort of a hold on her thoughts. On her emotions.

When she opened up, Finn cut a dark figure against the gritty, grey sky. He wore the collar of his jacket turned up, and a slight smirk on his lips. There was something there which Cassandra didn't quite like at first. To start with, she thought he might believe he had won some sort of a victory over her. In the end, though, she made peace with herself, trying to make herself forget her first impressions.

It was time for her to grow up.

She was going to be the mature person here.

The *adult*.

There was no need for Cassandra to say anything. Finn stepped right in, and she followed him to the kitchen. Before she had a chance to ask what he was doing here — why he had come to see her — he said, "I want to apologise. For not entering into the spirit of sharing. You know, not following through with the whole, 'show-you-mine-if-you'll-show-me-yours thing'."

Although she had imagined a more elegant apology than this, she supposed she should feel content he had seen fit to issue her one at all.

That was something, at least.

"And," Finn went on, as if he was worried she was going to jump in — rejecting his apology out of hand, "I'm willing to tell you what I'm up to . . . just what the project is that I'm working on. Would that be okay?"

Cassandra thought on this. Then something within her swelled up. It overwhelmed her. All logical thought left her behind.

She pushed herself into him, pressing their lips together.

She felt his intense warmth.

A severe heat.

He *burned* her.

Before Finn could quite catch his balance, she grabbed hold of him, taking the lapels of his jacket tightly in her fists. He wasn't going to get away.

Not this time.

Not *ever*.

As she pulled him in tighter, she took steps backwards, bringing the two of them closer and closer to the studio — to where she had so willingly shown him her beating heart. And where he had betrayed her trust.

Where he had betrayed the deal they had made.

She brought him in through the doorway, no longer caring about having left the sketches she had been working on out on the desktop for anybody to see. She possessed enough presence of mind — however — to bring the blinds down over the windows which looked out onto the street outside. That done, she could fully concentrate on Finn.

This time she took stock of the situation. She gave him some room to breathe.

A sporting chance.

She absorbed him standing before her, feeling as if he had never looked so handsome. As if he had never cut such a manly, in-control figure. Her heart thumped loudly in her throat, and her pulse tapped a rapid, uncontrollable rhythm at her temples.

It was now she realised he was staring unabashedly at the drawings she had been working on that morning. His eyes fixed upon them. Taking them in. As if he was intent on memorising each and every line and angle of what she had created. For what purpose he did such a thing, Cassandra truly had no idea.

In a rush of inspiration, she flapped out her arm and brushed the sketches from the desktop as if they had been nothing more significant than breadcrumbs — to be swept up at some later time. Then — turning her eyes onto Finn's startled expression — she realised it was time to seize back control.

She grabbed him around the hips, thrusting him into her, feeling his rigid, muscular body up against hers. A gasp slipped out from between his lips.

She kissed him again.

Long and slow.

Her hands continued to wander about his body, pausing at his pecs and his washboard stomach. She was certain he had some sort of rigorous hotel-room workout routine which he performed to preserve such an impressive physique. He certainly didn't seem the type who would frequent the gym.

Just as she would never have been seen dead in a gym.

Gently, she eased his shirt up over his torso.

She pressed her face into his hard flesh.

Felt the warmth of his skin.

And felt the shuddering rhythm of his heartbeat.

She guided him to the desk, to where her sketches had been lying until a few moments before. He made no protest, and put up no resistance. He was clearly glad to follow her lead. To submit to her.

She lay him down and stood over him.

His eyes remained locked on hers.

And his body stayed still.

As if he was afraid he might suffer some consequence should he so much as twitch.

"Your turn, I think," he said, with a slight smile.

All of a sudden, she felt very aware of herself. Of her own body. She took a step back then reached up to the top button of her blouse, as if the very idea she might undo it appalled her. She looked to his jeans, a smile sneaking onto her lips.

Finn held his resolve for a few more seconds before finally breaking down. He threw up his arms in surrender. He pulled down his trousers.

Cassandra watched on hungrily as they fell to the ground.

"Happy now?" he asked.

She felt something thaw in her. A warmth gripped her gut. She trod towards him, feeling as if she was performing on a smoky stage, in some cosy, underground theatre. It felt as if Finn was lying in the spotlight. As if he was the main attraction.

The feature presentation.

A shudder passed across the surface of her skin. She felt as if Finn's blood called out to hers. As if they were drawn together by some form of magnetism.

A naturally occurring bond.

Slowly — so slowly — she stripped.

This done, she enjoyed another few moments of domination. Allowing herself the pleasure of believing that she was all-powerful . . . that she could do anything she wished with this boy she had here. That she could bend him to her will.

All it required was her say-so.

All it required was her will to make it happen.

If she wished, she could back out of the studio.

Steal his clothes.

Lock him in here.

In the dark.

If he wanted to get out he would need to break a window.

Or bust the door.

The idea tantalised her.

And then sense cut in.

She turned her attention back down onto the man before her.

Why would she waste such a delicious opportunity?

Feeling as if she was the strongest force in the entire universe at that precise moment in time, she perched atop him, staring into his face through the bottoms of her eyes — feeling him tremble a little beneath her touch.

As she laid her bare breasts against his naked skin, she heard him gasp.

And utter words just beneath his breath.

Words which only she — a hair's width from his lips — would hear:

"I love you."

27

CAUGHT IN A SUMMER DAZE

"This way then!"

Finn tuned back into his surroundings.

He had got lost there.

Gone somewhere else entirely.

He snapped back to reality, to the sun which beamed across the fields, the trenches alive with activity. The somewhat surreal sight of a battalion of archaeologists working shovels into the earth, turning it over, hoping to reveal mysteries buried beneath.

Then he turned to the foreground, to Petunia Knightly who — as always — was too close to his earlobe for comfort. The ever-present grin fixed onto her lips.

"I think you should get a shot from the other side . . . that way the sun will be behind the shot. Wouldn't that work best?"

He thought through this comment, trying to make sense of it. In the end, he decided — with a little pain — that she was correct. To be quite honest, he was unsure why he was standing where he was . . . why he had ended up pointing his camera directly into the sun. It was all because of Cassandra. She was the one to blame. His mind had been somewhere else entirely. His lack of professionalism was appalling . . .

Feeling sweat seeping from just about every pore, he made gradual progress across the field to where Petunia had rightly instructed him would be the best vantage point for a landscape shot. He set up his tripod once again and worked the viewfinder — squeezing everything into the frame.

Even as he stood at the camera — even as he attempted to focus in on the less-than-gripping scene unfolding before him — he felt his concentration deserting him once more. He had told her that he loved her. That was what he had said.

A direct quote:

I love you.

There had been no foreplanning preceding the remark. He thought of past relationships, and about how he had spent weeks thinking things over . . . wondering whether this or that was the right time . . . and then . . . and then, he had never — *ever* — been the first one to say it. The other person had always beaten him to it.

But not this time.

Was that what rankled him?

Or was it the fact that Cassandra had said nothing in response?

That she hadn't said she loved him back?

What would he do if she *didn't* love him back?

"Finnie! Finnie!"

Once more, Finn was dragged back to the present.

To the field.

To the excavations.

To the Knightly twins.

And this project of theirs . . . whatever its intention was.

He looked up just in time to see Petunia approaching, as ever with Titania trailing in her wake. His heart sank — as it always did — just at the sight of them.

"We *were* wondering if you would conduct an interview with us."

"Another one?" Finn replied, without thinking his response through.

Petunia blinked rapidly a couple of times, and placed her hand on her hip. Her tone of voice was somewhat strained — hinting at impatience. "Well, if we are to give the viewers a fully fleshed-out idea of the whole situation then we'll need to have *plenty* of footage on the two of us, explaining the family history; that sort of thing."

Finn resisted the temptation to suggest that what they were really looking for was a family-historian-for-hire . . . someone who had the patience to listen to people's mundane stories about their heritage. Those stories which were riveting only to those who had any sort of personal stake in them.

However, deciding he should venture down the path of least resistance, Finn indulged Petunia. He even managed to put together a half-coherent chain of questions, to which Petunia gave very thorough — if not entirely *fleshed-out* — answers.

It was startling just how difficult it truly was to exhaust Petunia's patience when she was speaking about her own family. Whenever Finn made a hint at wrapping things up — in suggesting they had all they needed for the time being — Petunia would start off all over again on some other directionless tirade. By the time Petunia finally did stop speaking, he was so sure she was going to start again that he just gawped.

As he packed his camera away, he overheard one of the archaeologists calling out.

He ignored this cry to start with.

It had been his experience over the days he had spent here — at the site — that archaeologists could get excited about almost anything. Usually it was some muddy fragment of pottery, or else a rusted-up piece of metal. It was only when he had packed his camera away and was giving the scene a final look-over before heading back to Normonswold that he realised this time the excitement had cause.

Finn peeped over the heads of the archaeologists before him. He looked down to where they had been digging. He realised right away there was no sign of the archaeologist who had made the initial fuss . . . that that particular archaeologist had disappeared into the depths of the hole.

He looked about the others, overhearing one of them explain they had finally uncovered one of the entrances to the under-ground tunnels.

Finn felt the Knightly sisters close by. He expected to hear Petunia's shrill voice in his ear — imploring him to 'get his camera out' — but she remained just as stunned by the sight as everybody else.

Although he had been there when the archaeologists had confirmed the presence of the underground tunnels using their detectors, it felt an entirely different matter to be actually seeing one with his own eyes.

He listened in to the archaeologists ahead of him; both of them women. ". . . Probably forks about here, before heading off to the junction. This one right here'll go beneath the town — I bet you."

"How much?" the other archaeologist replied.

"A steak dinner."

"Deal."

Finn shifted his attention away from the hole. "What're you planning to do now, with this discovery?"

It felt almost as if he had belched, loudly, and without shame, in the middle of a black-tie dinner.

The two archaeologists turned on their heels and gawped.

Finally, one of them took pity on him.

"This is probably — *singlehandedly* — the greatest archaeological discovery of the century. At least in *this* country."

"And why's that?" he replied, cutting through the woman's arrogant tone.

The archaeologists exchanged glances. This time the other one answered. "These tunnels — the Piracy Passage — has been rumoured for centuries. They run from the east coast, in theory converging somewhere about here, before feeding all the way through to London where they fan out into a variety of secret exits." The archaeologist drew breath. "Nobody, though, has ever been able to discover whether or not they truly exist. When we ran the tests — a few weeks ago — we could see there was *something* beneath the land . . . but even then the most fervent believers among us doubted we had truly come across this great, unknown network of tunnels."

"And how can you be so sure this *is* what you're looking for?"

It was clear the archaeologists were doing their best not to sigh right in his face.

The first archaeologist spoke again. Her explanation was complete with arm gestures which were clearly reserved for when she went to schools to speak with children under the age of ten. "Because we've already sent a robot *down there* with an infrared camera. We've scoped out the structure and come across one of the junctions. The one from which all of the passages converge. If this was some sort of a secret passageway into the nearby village then there would never have been any reason for such complication. And — of course — the passageway would've stopped here, rather than continuing on to the coast."

Finn thought about this for several moments. Although everything within him told him just to stay silent, that he was only wasting his time to further test these archaeologists' patience, he couldn't help himself.

"So, you're saying that the tunnels from the coast all converge here — beneath what was once the Knightly Estate —"

Here Petunia — apparently eavesdropping — pitched in. "I think you'll find that it *continues* to be the Knightly Estate."

Finn turned back to the archaeologists, intent on getting his question out before Petunia hijacked the conversation. "After the tunnels meet beneath the Knightly Estate, they then become one central tunnel and head off to London?"

The archaeologist put on a firm smile and nodded — perhaps at last acknowledging that Finn wasn't a total dim bulb.

"And the tunnel passes *beneath* the village? Beneath Normonswold?"

"Correct," the archaeologist replied. "As I already alluded, the job for us is now to establish that this tunnel does in fact lead to London."

"Do you have any idea of the route it would take, beyond Normonswold?"

"There are maps," the other archaeologist replied. "But they are crude, and of course the terrain has changed over the centuries. It will be a long project."

"But a well-funded one!" the first archaeologist put in.

Finn couldn't help but sense the tone of enthusiasm in the archaeologist's voice when she said this. Then again, he supposed that everybody in the world constantly strove for a sense of job security. He was no different, of course.

Somewhat painfully, Petunia spoke up again. "You already have my permission to tear up whatever you will. This land should be for heritage — there should be no impediment where the clarification and detailing of history is concerned."

Finn couldn't help thinking that he wasn't entirely convinced by the absolute nature of this statement. He turned his attention back to the archaeologists. "You would need to knock down the leisure resort Lord Charles built?"

"Oh, absolutely," the archaeologist said, with no small amount of glee.

"And I cannot help but feel a touch sorry for those in the village nearby . . . in Norfichold —"

"*Normonswold.*"

"Yes, yes," the archaeologist continued. "Once government money comes into play the village will be on limited time. Not long at all before compulsory purchase orders start popping up."

This was the only moment in the conversation — if that was what it could be called — where the archaeologists exchanged anything approaching a sisterly glance. The first archaeologist gave the one who had just made the comment about the 'compulsory purchase orders' a fiery glare.

In answer to the assumed criticism, the archaeologist who had just spoken flushed slightly, averted her gaze, and then looked back at Finn. "Of course, this is all speculation for the time being. We would need to get the funding first. And there would be a *long* wait before anybody had any reason to believe their home was under threat."

This, however, felt like too little too late.

He kept himself cool, as he had learned to do throughout many years of filming in far more incendiary situations. "Of course," he replied, smiling, happy to step back into the role of the fool the archaeologists had placed him in.

The archaeologists turned their attention back to the hole before them, and — seeing Petunia was chewing the ear off her twin sister Titania about something or other — Finn took the opportunity to break away.

When he got out of the field, and set foot on the sure asphalt of the road, he broke into a run. He wasn't sure why. It was a childish reaction.

He just felt he had to escape.

And fast.

28

TEA PARTY

*T*he warm smell of cooking pastry wafted in beneath the door.

Cassandra blinked herself around from the nap she had been taking on the sofa in the studio. She knew it had been a bad idea to allow Bella to convince her a sofa would help to complete the room. It was nothing but a lewd temptation. Whenever Cassandra felt her creative forces flagging — her resilience dipping — her gaze would always shift off in the direction of the sofa, and she would think about lying down 'just for five minutes' . . . and maybe draping the soft, velvety blanket over her . . . and 'just closing her eyes for a few seconds, nothing more' . . . and before she knew it, she would slip off to the Land of Nod — only coming to several hours later.

Just like it had happened now.

She stretched out the crick in her neck. She had been sleeping without dreaming. Just a wonderful, blank canvas in her mind. Although in her youth she had often thought of naps as being something for either the old or the sick, she had recently come around to their important restorative effect. It was true that whenever she had had a nap of an hour or so, she woke with a new sense of balance in her mind.

As if she had had a chance to unclutter her consciousness from all that had taken place that day. As if her life was cluttered or complicated at all . . .

She looked over to the drawings she had produced that morning, impressed at the pile she had created for Bella to scrutinise. She hadn't slacked off. She had done the work she had needed to get done. And yet a sense of guilt clung to her.

She got up and looked herself over in the full-length mirror she and Bella had had installed. Although she was willing to admit the sofa could've been done away with, there was no circumstance under which she could think of not allowing the mirror into the studio. There had been so many snap visits by this person or the other . . . where the prospect of sneaking upstairs to her bedroom — to check on her appearance — was rendered utterly impossible.

She could certainly hear unfamiliar voices coming from the kitchen.

It was a compromise.

Something of a gamble.

Although she had little enthusiasm for speaking with anybody except for perhaps Bella, or someone else from Humble, there was no denying the attraction freshly baked pastry presented.

On the inside of the locked studio door, she remained genuinely torn, wondering if she might be able to risk sneaking out some time later — when everyone had gone . . . but by then there might not be any pastries left!

Finally, she was bold.

She turned the door handle and stepped out into the real world.

***

The smell emanating from the kitchen only became more delightful the closer she got. The thick, rich smell of chocolate wafted up her nostrils and her heart swelled in her throat. There was something about chocolate which elicited a feeling that was something like love . . . warm, and gooey, and impossibly sweet . . .

No sooner had she stepped through the kitchen doorway than she took stock of Bella, Robert, Indigo and Peter all sitting around the table. They all had a cup of tea and nobody was speaking. Because she had always been happy to relegate social niceties to second place — at least when it came to sugary treats — Cassandra turned her attention onto the pain au chocolat, pain aux raisins, and croissants steaming away gently in the basket on the table.

It was one of those situations where everybody was clearly looking for any reason — any reason *at all* — to break the uncomfortable silence. And Cassandra walking onto the scene was the perfect excuse.

"Cass-*andra!*" Indigo Miles declared, rising from her seat, rounding the table, and then giving her a kiss on either cheek while she firmly grasped her shoulders. "If it isn't the most wonderful *illustrator* in the whole of the village."

She had always somewhat disliked the word 'illustrator' — it had a scientific bent. But she wasn't about to argue the point right now. Not when things were clearly so awkward. Not when there were delicious pastries to consume.

She pressed on a smile and did her best to look everybody around the table in the eye. She found this particularly difficult in the case of Bella, who was clearly not having a good time with her mother and her beau du jour.

Cassandra sat at the table. She felt only slightly recompensed for the discomfort of the atmosphere by the cup of tea and pain-au-chocolat placed in front of her.

Everybody fully focused on her, clearly having been waiting for a good conversation piece. She squeezed the handle of her cup, reaching the point where she was afraid she might snap the porcelain in two.

Apparently wishing to cut through — or even completely ignore — the discomfort which lingered, Peter spoke. "Bella was just telling us how you are putting the finishing touches to a whole new line of cards — an *autumn* collection."

Truth be told, since it seemed that spring had only just finished, and that summer had barely begun, Cassandra had found creating the autumnal cards something of a struggle. In the past, she and Bella had reached a mutual decision that they would always be creating cards during the actual season that they corresponded to with the idea that they would be ready for sale that time next year. However, the wheels had soon come off these good intentions. They had got behind schedule.

And they were a little over six months behind now.

All the same, she did her best to smile. "That's right" — she shifted a glance off in Bella's direction — "has Bella told you anything about it?"

"Oh, no," Peter replied, puffing out his cheeks, and then breaking into a grin once again. "To tell the truth, she has been somewhat tight-lipped about the whole operation. It's almost as if it's some top-secret project."

She wanted to respond that this was as she wished it to be in an ideal world but her manners prevented such an indiscrete statement.

Peter glanced about the table and Cassandra knew exactly what would be coming next. "So, could we see some of the designs?"

Cassandra shot off an involuntary glare across the table at Bella.

Seemingly preoccupied with the current situation, and ready to throw anybody under the bus to save herself, Bella averted her gaze.

Cassandra breathed in sharply, glanced down at her untested tea and pain-au-chocolat, and decided she had little choice. She got up, dipped into her studio, and riffled through her latest set of sketches, all the time swearing to herself under her breath.

In the end, she slipped out a few Bella had already seen, and approved of. As she marched towards the kitchen, she couldn't help but feel quite pleased with the sketches. Her gloomy mood lifted somewhat as she handed them over to Peter for inspection.

She did her best to act normally, bringing her lukewarm tea up to her lips and sipping. She took a bite out of her pain-au-choco-lat, glad to find it was as agreeable as it had smelled. She watched Peter's expression as he looked through the sketches.

A smile snaked across his lips. He glanced up from the current drawing. "Why," he said, "this looks familiar. This is Pawler's Bay, is it not?"

Mouth full of pain-au-chocolat, Cassandra nodded.

"Remarkable," he continued, "and you've set the scene in autumn — the bracken beginning to die . . . the grasses thinning . . . turning brown."

Indigo peered over Peter's arm, eyes screwed up, scrutinising. "I don't know how you can *possibly* tell the grass is turning brown.

The drawing is in black and white." She glanced up. "Have you ever thought of using colour in your work?"

Feeling under attack, Cassandra sank back in her chair. "Sometimes I do — it depends."

"Then this is unfinished?" Indigo continued then exchanged glances with Peter.

Peter took up her defence. "I would say, my dear, that it is entirely up to the artist to decide whether or not to use colour. I was merely remarking on the fact that the sketch is so realistically rendered so as to give the *impression* of colour."

"Ha!" Indigo said.

Cassandra felt her stomach tighten. She looked to Bella.

Still she didn't step in.

Indigo sat up, leaning her head back so she could better look down her nose at all of them. "It's only a short trip down *this* route before we start talking about how the viewer has to imagine *everything* — sooner or later we'll all be staring at a blank page!"

A sense of outrage filled her. A kind of twisting, almost violent fury. She balled her fists down at her thighs. And began to tremble.

"Now, now, Indigo," Peter said — and Cassandra thought he was on the point of wagging his finger, "you know that is a deceptive argument —"

"I'm just stating the obvious!" Indigo replied, her voice rising to a shriek.

Cassandra cast a glance in Bella's direction, as if it was her place to control her mother — as if the role of mother and daughter had been reversed . . .

Then, because there seemed nothing else to be done, she cast a look at Robert, acknowledging the two of them were the closest to being neutrals in this conflict.

Robert, however, merely gave her a sympathetic half-smile.

Indigo had risen from her seat now. She grasped the edge of the table, assuming a catlike posture, as if she planned to spring upon Peter at a moment of her choosing.

Cassandra desperately cast around for a reason to excuse herself.

An explosion.

Smoke.

Sirens.

Something.

. . . But — this being Normonswold — not one of those welcome interruptions was forthcoming.

Indigo continued her tirade. "I am *so* fed up of feeling *stupid* about everything."

Cassandra looked to Bella, again hoping she might step in.

But she didn't move a muscle.

Indigo stepped away from the kitchen table.

For a moment, Cassandra was convinced she was only doing this so she might get a run-up to leap upon Peter. But she held her ground. It was then that Cassandra noticed a tear was snaking a path down Indigo's cheek.

It clung to her chin for a second or so before dropping to the floor.

And then — without another word — Indigo turned on her heel and marched out of Molinaar's Cottage, slamming the front door.

A silence descended upon the kitchen.

Peter's alarmed expression spoke for all of them.

Mumbling something or other under his breath, he rose to his feet, and then — almost tripping over twice — excused himself and made off after her, bringing the front door shut with a far more measured *click*.

As the scene cleared — as Cassandra's heartrate returned to something like its normal rhythm — the sense of outrage she had felt came bubbling to the surface. She turned to Bella, ready to unleash her anger.

Bella, however, was smiling grimly.

This disarmed her.

"Cass," Bella said, getting up and embracing her. "I'm *so* sorry. I didn't mean for you to be collateral damage. But I needed to do something. There was no other way."

From her position in Bella's embrace, Cassandra looked over her shoulder, to Robert. He was smirking, giving her a knowing glance. He was clearly as unconvinced about Bella's supposed strategy as Cassandra.

Bella backed out of the hug. "I just needed things to blow up about *something* . . . this seemed the easiest way . . . it was cheap and it was *nasty* . . . but it was something I could *guarantee* working . . . I'd overheard them speaking about something similar, and I knew if I raked things up . . . just a *little*, then everything would spill over."

She tried to find comfort in Bella's explanation, but still felt the same sense of outrage. She had been used . . . there wasn't any other way to describe it.

In the end, though, Robert spoke. "Remind me, Bella, just why you're so keen for your mother and Peter the Director to break up?"

Bella remained very still.

Cassandra thought she saw some expression pass over her face — some trace of the mania which so often erupted in her mother, Indigo Miles.

But then it was gone.

"I . . . it's not right — that's all . . . they're not right for one another."

Robert gave a sigh, and then looked about, as if searching for Woss.

Woss, though, had had more sense than Cassandra. He had made himself scarce long before this scene had reached its climatic phase.

Robert shifted his attention back onto Bella. "Who will be right for your mother?" he asked. "Why don't you just let her make her mind up?"

Bella remained where she was, undecided whether or not she should be vexed by this comment. In the end, she just stood where she was, in shock.

Unwilling to let the chance slip through her fingers when it was so neatly presented, Cassandra popped the last piece of pain-au-chocolat between her lips, knocked back the last of her tea, then ventured out of the kitchen.

As she brought the studio door shut behind her, she heard the gentle mumble of Robert's voice, followed by Bella's muffled sobs.

29

GOVERNMENT OFFICIALS

*A*s Finn stood behind his camera, he wasn't quite sure what to make of the scene. He watched on as a large vehicle — a van with tinted windows — barrelled its way across the course, muddy path of the field, making a beeline for the entrance to the tunnels which the archaeologists had opened up.

As always happened at times like this, Finn thought about turning off his camera. He suppressed the momentary, panicked urge, and then began to feel somewhat excited. Every time he had experienced the sensation, he had made a point of leaving his camera on. And each time he was rewarded. Even if he ended up unable to use his footage later on — and that was often the case — he would be able to revisit the moments in private. And everything would build towards the project as he regarded it in his mind.

He peered over the top of his camera, watching as the figures in formal business dress descended from the car. All in black, with sunglasses on, they all looked as if they were ready for a funeral.

The scene was made further absurd by the fact they were all —
somehow — wearing wellington boots. It seemed they had
performed their research before setting out on their journey.

Government officials.

There was no other explanation.

Deciding he could lose nothing by getting a bit closer, he swept
his camera up — tripod and all — and headed towards the people
who had just arrived. They were in deep conversation with the
woman who Finn recognised as being the lead archaeologist. He
couldn't yet see any sign of Petunia or Titania, and he supposed
they were still coming around in their suite at the leisure complex
on the field adjacent.

When Finn was close enough to overhear the conversation, he
left the camera recording but kept it pointed at the ground. He
stood by idly, making a point of putting a bemused expression on
his face, as if anything he might overhear would be completely lost
on him. As if he was just some clueless bystander.

Which — he supposed, in many ways — he was.

The suited people spoke in hurried tones with the archaeologist, and Finn soon lost his way in the conversation, although he
understood the overriding topic.

They were discussing the exact route of the tunnels.

And precisely in the local area.

One of the people who had arrived produced a camera and
commenced taking pictures. When she shifted her attention onto
him, she paused.

Finn was certain they hadn't come here to photograph clumps
of muddy ground. He knew — as in all cases like these — that
whoever had sent these people would like to have a full view of
matters.

The Big Picture.

Everybody involved.

It was only after the camerawoman had left him behind, and the people were led away by the lead archaeologist to what had once been the Knightly Leisure Resort that he wondered whether or not they would have the capability to match up the photo they had taken with his likeness on some database.

If they did, what would they find?

He thought about it a few moments.

Then let the thought go.

There were so many things he had been involved with down the years — what some might call 'controversy'.

But it wasn't like this was some kind of criminal investigation or anything.

Not yet, anyway.

He trod past the parked car, unable to help himself trying the door handle, to see if they had left it unlocked. They hadn't. He couldn't help but give a slight smile at this — at his old, investigative nature. He supposed he could end up in a place as backwater as Normonswold and yet he would go on possessing his investigative spirit forever.

He waited around for another twenty minutes or so, making himself busy with the tunnels, taking as much footage as he could manage. When he was through with that, he noticed the officials were returning from the leisure complex.

Again keeping his camera down by his side, he watched on as they passed through the trees, approaching him.

He couldn't help his attention falling upon the official with the camera once more, glad to see she was uninterested in taking photos of him . . . as if she might've flagged him up earlier on as being some sort of 'undesirable'.

After another brief conversation, the officials got back into the van, and — with a thundering *growl* — they set off again.

Once they had slipped from view, Finn approached the lead archaeologist.

"How did the meeting go?" he asked.

She grinned back — her smile showing off slightly wonky teeth. "Great. Well . . . it was about what we expected."

"And what did you expect?"

"Oh, you know, all the usual terms and conditions. They gave us a heads-up about what to expect through the post. About what the drawn-up documents will say. It was a useful meeting." She held Finn's stare for another moment, as if assessing whether or not to trust him with what she was going to say next. "They said that we're going to need to tear up that whole complex in the next field over. You know, where we've been staying. And then there's all the stuff with the village to sort out."

"What stuff with the village?"

Finn had given himself away a little with his sharp tone.

However, after a brief glance-around, the archaeologist responded.

"CPOs."

"Compulsory purchase orders?"

She glowered then dropped her voice to a whisper. "Uh-huh."

"You mean they're going to take charge of the village?"

"Knock it all down, probably. If this discovery turns out to be as significant as we believe it is." With this, she was called away by one of her team.

Finn felt his ribs tighten over his heart and lungs. He looked about, feeling a numbness creeping through him. Every instinct told him to run to Normonswold, to deliver the news personally. And then he looked back across the fields and wondered whether that was really a good idea. Nothing had been *confirmed* yet.

There was still time.

And then another thought struck him.

If there was just some way to pull it off. . .

30

WILDERNESS SURPRISE

*C*assandra slung her rucksack over her shoulder and ventured out of Molinaar's Cottage. Her rucksack contained a fresh pair of clothes, a toothbrush, and some other overnight essentials. That was all Finn had asked her to pack.

The sun was just dipping down beneath the horizon, and the streetlights were beginning to blink on, shedding their eerie, yellowish glow all about the quaint main street of Normonswold. She felt her heart jig in her chest, the stirring sense of adventure in her stomach. As she walked through the streets, she tuned into the birdsong, and the gentle *rustle* of the breeze through the leaves. The whole scene was so tranquil. It sent warm waves rippling through her. She couldn't remember a time when she felt quite so at peace with herself; and her life.

Soon after the dramatic scene featuring Bella's mother and her beau — Peter — Bella had come to Cassandra to apologise for using her to bait an argument between the two of them. Bella explained that — if it was any consolation — the argument that her sketch had invoked had failed to force the desired effect . . . the separation of the couple.

She had accepted Bella's apology, and had decided to put the matter behind her. In any case, she knew she had to be less precious about allowing the world into her studio — into her *art* . . . she had taken the decision to put her work out there so she should be willing to accept the consequences.

There came a time when a mother had to allow her baby to go free.

To — for better or worse — stand on its own two feet.

She felt like whistling as she made her way along the back country lanes leading away from Normonswold. This was nothing like the time when she had attempted to sneak away from the world; to escape her anxieties merely by putting distance between herself and them. This time Finn had invited her to meet him in the countryside.

At a specific spot.

The gate leading into a field which'd belonged — still belonged? — to Lord Charles. One of those growing fallow beside what had been the Knightly Leisure Complex.

As she closed in on the agreed location, she couldn't help thinking just how little she truly thought about the countryside which surrounded her on all sides. She supposed it should make her feel trapped, or unashamedly free . . . but — in the end — it had neither effect. She had no reason to think about it at all on a daily basis. When she went about her daily routine. When she had her daily work to get done.

The moon was just peeping out from behind wispy cloud as she crunched over the gravelly path leading into the field. In the fading, yellowy light of the sunset, it felt as if magic hung in the air. As if there was some fiery current linking every living thing.

And then she set eyes on Finn.

He was sitting hunched-up on a stone wall, hands clasped together, his jacket draped about his shoulders. When she noticed him, he straightened up, then rose. He had clearly heard her approaching — if he hadn't been able to see her clearly making progress along the countryside path. He wore a great smile as he took stock of her.

Her heart beat against her throat.

And her whole body went numb.

"You didn't get lost in the wilderness, then?" he asked, kissing her softly on the lips.

"Why, was this supposed to be some sort of test?"

"If it was, then you definitely passed . . . there was no reason to call in Mountain Rescue, in any case."

"I didn't realise Mountain Rescue covered parts of the country with hills no larger than a hundred metres."

"You'd be surprised at what they do cover."

She lightly prised them apart. She looked out over the field, able to see the silhouettes of the abandoned leisure complex beyond. "This place is a bit eerie, to be honest. You know, kind of like it's been forgotten by everybody. If it was just the two of us still in existence on the surface of the Earth, I'd imagine it looking just like this."

"How'd you know the world hasn't ended in the time you took to get here?"

"I don't. And I guess I won't know for sure until I get back to the village."

"Are you ready to see what I want to show you?"

"Well, that's a self-defeating question, if I ever heard one. I have no idea what you want to show me."

He broke into a grin. "Then you'll just have to trust me."

They passed through the first field — the one closest the road — winding their way along the dirt track and then through a copse.

Along the way, Finn produced a pair of torches, and handed one over to her. The two of them shone their bright circles of light over the scene ahead. She was immediately alerted to the broken ground on all sides. It made her think they were ploughing the field, but it was the wrong time of year. And there was a chaotic pattern to it — if there was any pattern at all . . . great, big clods of mud here and there.

As if they were digging holes.

"This way," Finn said, taking her by the arm, gently guiding her away from the firm underfooting of the dirt path.

They ventured onto the muddy field.

With each step, Cassandra felt more and more earth sticking to her walking boots. She was glad that she had gone with proper footwear tonight — that she hadn't for some reason opted for a pair of sexy high heels; although if she had asked Bella her advice that was probably how she would've ended up . . .

She wanted to ask Finn questions — about what it meant. However, her mind was thoroughly occupied with merely navigating the terrain without one of her feet slipping and sinking into a hole. She had no intention of turning her ankle out here, even in the company of a gallant specimen of a man such as Finn.

"Over here," he said, motioning her over to a particular hole.

The two of them stood at the edge, peering down into the gloom.

When Finn began to shine his torch into the darkness, Cassandra decided to do the same. She could see nothing but the clods of dirt below.

"Is this . . . where we're sleeping tonight?" she asked, unable to hold herself back.

Finn chuckled. "No, no. I've sorted out our accommodation in the next field over."

"Oh, I see, is it a much more comfortable hole?"

He sniggered. "Yeah, a much more comfortable one." He stepped up onto the muddy bank, reaching for her hand. "Come on, let's go down and take a look."

She was dubious. She looked down into the hole, and then to Finn. She thought of all the news stories she had read over the years of people getting into trouble when doing stupid things — *just like this!* — in the dark, in the middle of nowhere.

All the same, she allowed him to help her down into the hole.

When the two of them stood at the bottom, shining their torches in the darkness, she couldn't help but ask the question. "Uh, what're we supposed to be looking at?"

"This," Finn said, bringing the torch up near his face so = she could see he wore a wicked grin, "is what's known as the Piracy Passage." He brushed off a muddy layer from the tunnel ceiling to reveal a wooden beam beneath. "See?"

"What's the 'Piracy Passage'?"

"It's a route through which goods were smuggled in from the coast and taken underground all the way to London."

She looked into the darkness of the tunnel. "You mean this leads to London?"

"Actually, that way heads to the coast." He turned on the spot, still grinning, no doubt feeling extremely pleased with himself. "*This* way leads to London."

"Back to Normonswold?"

"Yes."

"Are there any exits into the village?"

"We don't know yet."

" 'We' ?"

"Well, you don't think I've been coming out here with a bucket and spade, making all of this mess myself, do you?"

"No, I suppose not."

"Come on," he said, stepping his way up the side of the muddy slope, and then reaching to help her out. "I'll show you what I mean."

The two of them headed away from the largest hole they had been exploring and made their way across the field, to the path leading into the next. There was something familiar about this route, although it didn't quite twig until she had made it through to the other side. Until she saw what had once been the Knightly Leisure Complex.

Low-lying buildings riddled the landscape. Once manicured gardens overspilled their plots. A little way beyond, she could see long grasses. It was more like a field of wheat than a golf course. She couldn't help but notice there were several lights lit within the buildings. It made her think of people who left the lights on in their houses so potential burglars might think there was someone at home.

Was that Lord Charles's intention?

She looked back at Finn. She felt impossibly stupid when she asked, "Aren't we trespassing?"

Finn shrugged. "I suppose so." Then he broke into a smile.

There was something about his manner which she found slightly unsettling. She couldn't quite put her finger on exactly what it was, though.

The two of them approached the main lodge of the resort.

Although the main lights weren't on, there was a dim white light from a lamp which shod a gentle glow across the path leading up to the door.

Finn went first, not missing a beat as he pushed on inside.

Cassandra dragged a moment, before reminding herself that Lord Charles was in the past . . . that the residents of Normonswold had sent him packing.

Were she and Finn about to discover him sitting alone in some room, like some sort of Colonel Kurtz, turned crazy in this wilderness of his own creating? However, as she navigated the corridors of the leisure complex, there were only mundane signs of neglect — dusty surfaces, mouse droppings, cobwebs.

Finn apparently knew where they were headed.

And it was all Cassandra could do to keep up.

He led them through various courtyards.

Each and every time, she tilted her head up to examine the glittering night sky. The stars were so clear out in the fields . . . even clearer than in Normonswold.

Finally, Finn brought them through a labyrinth of corridors. They passed through several security doors which he dismissed with the wave of a security card against a scanner. Where had he acquired the card? Had he broken in ahead of time?

After passing through yet another security door, they emerged in a round room, windows on every side. This gave a vista of the surrounding area . . . of the fields outside. When she looked up, she saw stars through the glass ceiling. When she eventually switched her attention back to her surroundings — to the room itself — she couldn't help but notice that the place was immaculately clean.

That whereas the rest of the resort was in a state of decay, this suite had been well-preserved . . . or perhaps it was just that *someone* had taken the time to give it a good cleaning.

The suite itself was tastefully enough furnished, with a sofa, table and chairs. Then there was the not-so-small matter of the four-poster bed. This reminded her of the castle where they had gone to visit Kareema Ashburton the year before.

She realised he was looking to her for some sign of approval. She locked onto his eyes, smiled wide, and said, "It's wonderful."

"And the view?"

"It's . . . great," she replied, looking out over the surrounding field.

"And it's all about to go away."

"What'd you mean?"

Here Finn produced a remote control. He jabbed a button and a mechanical *whirring* noise came from all around. Blinds slid into place over the windows.

Her heart thrummed in her throat.

When the blinds had finally slipped into place, she realised an array of lights had gently glowed into life, offering a new, warm light within the suite. She felt a slight sense of loss to have cut off the moonlight from outside. There was a question of privacy to consider, too . . . even if it was just from the heavens.

Although she wanted to explore the rest of the suite — to peep into the bathroom to see what sorts of wonders might await her — she felt herself becoming increasingly drawn into Finn. There was something about him . . . something which stole her breath.

Which entirely absorbed her.

As she reached up to run her fingers through his hair, she had to ask the question. She couldn't be afraid. "Were you telling the truth when you said you loved me?"

Finn twitched slightly. He drew back a little, so she could peer directly into his eyes. "What do you think?"

"I . . . guess there's no way for me to be sure."

"How'd I know that you love me?"

She smirked then pulled him tight. "If you have to ask, you'll never know."

He stepped back. "I want to stay in Normonswold. I *want* to stay here. With you."

She stared into his eyes. She felt as if the whole weight of his body passed through his stare. She felt him overwhelming her.

Overpowering her.

"Okay," she replied, and then took a step forward.

Another.

"Okay," she said, laying her hand upon his shoulder then gently sliding it up the side of his neck before coming to his tender cheek. She pressed her palm against his skin for the longest time, feeling the gentle *throb* of his heartbeat. Then she leaned into him, laid her lips against his.

He kissed her back.

And his arms wrapped around her.

She felt him lift up the back of her jumper, bringing it up slowly but surely.

She focused on him.

On his kiss.

On his body.

His beautiful hair.

She focused on just *being* with him.

As their passion became more frenzied, she felt herself being swept away.

She hoped this wasn't a great mistake.

A DIVINE MORNING — TAINTED

$\mathcal{W}$hen Cassandra stirred, she was lost for several seconds.

She looked around, confused by the dazzling daylight. To begin with — for some reason — she thought she might've died and gone to heaven. That would certainly go some way to explaining the events of the previous night . . .

When she realised she was alone, she picked up on the scent of coffee. She looked about, finally working out the smell wafted through the doorway opposite the bed.

It was then that Finn appeared, bearing a pair of cups.

She propped herself on her elbows so she would have a better view.

A sleepy smile drooping from his lips, Finn passed over her cup of coffee, and perched on the edge of the mattress. Bella took the coffee from him, taking several moments to breathe in the bitter, satisfying odour. She wondered when she had experienced the aroma of coffee for the first time. No doubt it had been back when she'd been a child. She had only begun to drink and enjoy it once she had been much older, but now it was a daily staple. The two of them sat and drank their coffee in silence.

She wondered if they had run out of things to say.

Was that damning for their relationship?

She hoped not . . .

It was only when they had finished, and Finn had taken her cup from her, and then clasped his hands about hers, that she realised there might be something going on. There was a slightly pained expression in Finn's eyes . . . as if there was something within him which was baying to escape.

"I should have told you this earlier," Finn said. "But I've been working with the Knightly twins. They approached me, about making a documentary. I . . . well, the first time I met them, I had no idea who they were. And then . . . they brought me to this field. They showed me what remained of this place."

Cassandra felt her pulse throbbing at her temple. She was putting all of the pieces together in a hurry. Trying to make sense of all of the fragments.

It was too much to take in all at once.

Why was Finn dumping all this on her right now?

Why hadn't he said anything *earlier*?

But she managed to hold her concentration.

She would hear him out.

"So we're not trespassing after all?" she asked.

Finn shook his head. "I've been filming the progress of the tunnels — of their excavations. It's been, well, more interesting than I thought it would be. But in the past week things have got sort of . . . I don't know . . . more complicated?"

" 'Complicated' how?"

"Uh, well, when they started, the twins took me on with the

understanding that everything I did would be regarded as confidential. And that was fine. I suppose I never really appreciate what'd gone on with Lord Charles earlier, although I know you mentioned it a couple of times . . . but I never expected to be doing anything other than filming their stories and then sending them a kind of mock-up once I was done." He paused. "They pay me very well."

"What's become 'complicated' ?"

"Well, I showed you those tunnels. You remember, from yesterday?"

She wanted to stop Finn from stalling, but she had to be patient. "Uh-huh."

"And I said that it's the archaeologists' belief that the main tunnel switches back, runs beneath Normonswold?"

"Yes."

"The archaeologists say the government is planning to buy up the land, for further investigation. They are going to order people in Normonswold to give up their homes."

She took several seconds to absorb this fact. Then she cast another glance across the field, trying her best to get the idea through her mind. The fact that Finn had been secretly consorting with the Knightly twins — with Lord Charles's sisters. And then that he hadn't said a word about these tunnels until now.

She felt her cheeks heat up.

Blood pump to her temples.

"You do realise what this will mean for Bella, don't you? . . . For Humble?"

Finn stared at her. His mouth latched open a little.

"You have no idea how hard she fought against Lord Charles, his development plans. Normonswold means everything to her. It's her home — her *family* home. And Bella is my *business* partner."

Still, Finn didn't seem to get it.

She had the urge to shake him, but she held in the feeling, squeezing the words between her teeth. "There is *no way* — no way at all — that you will be able to stay in Normonswold if you continue to work with the Knightly twins. And even if you do stay, there will be no way we can keep going with . . ." feeling helpless, she waved her hand weakly ". . . with whatever it is we have going along here. It would affect me and Bella. As they say in business-speak, it would be 'acrimonious to positive relations'." Although she did her best to raise a smile, it died instantly upon her lips.

There was a long silence between the two of them.

It was Finn who broke it in the end.

"What do I need to do?" he asked.

She shook her head, smiled slightly, bemused he was even asking the question. "I'm saying if we're to stay together, you have to give up the documentary — whatever it is you're working on with the Knightly sisters."

"Or?"

"Or, I'll need . . . to go." As she uttered the last words, her throat constricted. She felt a slight stirring at the corners of her eyes, tears threatening to sneak free.

Finn held still for a long time, staring at his empty coffee cup. "Can't I finish what I started? I've made a contract . . ."

"Then get out of it," she replied, her tone of voice fierce.

Even as she heard her own words in her ears, she couldn't help wondering if she wasn't being needlessly overwrought. But she reminded herself that it wasn't just her and Bella who she was putting on the line by threatening their harmonious relations . . . there was Robert, Harriet and George to think about too — they all earned their living from Humble Greetings.

"I . . . can't . . ."

Rage blazed through Cassandra. "Yes, you can."

"I ..."

Before Finn could say anything further, Cassandra stormed from the suite — out of the Knightly Leisure Resort. It was only when she got to the road that she allowed herself to fully break free.

When tears streaked her cheeks she broke into a run.

32

MIND-MAPPING

*C*assandra spent most of the following days in near-solitude.

She would've thought that the trauma of the parting from Finn would've meant her creativity would retreat within her . . . but it was the complete opposite.

When she set pencil to paper, it was only hours later she surfaced. When she began to feel the muscular strains at her wrist and along her forearm. She scribbled stacks and stacks of pages for Bella to look over. On a few occasions, she found herself looking out of the window, to the street outside, half-expecting to see Finn strolling past.

But there was no sign of him.

He had made up his mind.

He had made his choice.

The most important thing for him was to finish the project he was working on. The most important thing for Cassandra was her work.

The two of them had simply taken different paths.

That was all.

Several times, she had wondered about breaking the news to Bella. But she might end up frightening her for no reason. The truth of the matter was that Finn had only suggested the government was *thinking* of buying up the village of Normonswold . . . but she hadn't pressed him for further information. And Bella would surely want to know everything about it. But that would mean Cassandra speaking with Finn again.

And she couldn't count on that.

She told herself there was no alternative but to put it off for the time being.

And then — one day — a letter landed on the doormat.

She was sitting at the kitchen table, sipping at her coffee. She trotted along with Woss to where the letter had landed, beating him to it.

The envelope was addressed to the Occupier.

She slit it open and slipped out the folded-up letter.

Her heart beat against her throat as she scanned the text.

As she realised its meaning.

An official government notification.

That their home was to be placed under compulsory purchase order, and that this demand was to be made on the basis of the preservation of national heritage.

Over her shoulder, she heard the stairs creaking.

Something froze within her, and she quickly slipped the letter into her pocket.

When she turned on the spot, she was certain her expression gave her away.

Robert and Bella entered the kitchen.

"Cass!" Bella said. "We're going to Old Couples' Café. Are you coming?"

Cassandra felt the weight of the letter in her pocket. She had the urge to slip it out and give it to Bella right there and then.

But she didn't.

Old Couples' Café was just off Normonswold High Street. The walls hadn't changed in the past thirty years. Neither had the furniture.

Bella picked out a sofa and a group of armchairs over in the corner. This was Cassandra's favourite spot — the one she picked out whenever she came in here alone. She liked to be able to spread her sketches over the coffee table.

Once Cassandra had descended into the armchair, she found herself looking over the photographs nailed to the walls. Photographs of the couple who owned the café — Geoff and Dee. The photos featured the two of them in various locales around the world. There was something which tickled her about the fact that Geoff and Dee had once been globe-trotters. She couldn't imagine either one of them leaving Normonswold for more than a few days.

When they had all settled in, she still felt deeply aware of the letter in her pocket. But Bella and Robert were laughing and smiling, and it seemed a shame to ruin the moment, so she stayed silent. It was only when she looked up and saw Indigo and Peter — walking arm in arm — making their way down the street outside that she realised just what she had got herself in for. Panicked now, she looked to Bella.

"Really," Bella said, with a smile. "It's all right. I promise all the fireworks are done with." As Indigo and Peter crossed the threshold of the café, Bella added, under her breath, "At least *I'm* not going to be the one stirring up the coals this time."

Cassandra waited for Indigo's greeting.

But it never came.

Instead, she lurched between all of them, and slapped something down on the table. It took Cassandra only a moment to register what it was.

Indigo had received the same letter.

All of them craned their necks to look.

Then Bella spoke.

"What is it?"

"Read it — just *read* it!" Indigo replied.

Bella did as she was told. As did Robert.

Cassandra held herself back.

She was deeply aware of the letter still in her pocket.

Why hadn't she said anything?

Why hadn't she just handed the letter over to Bella in the first place?

Why was she so intent on *not* upsetting her?

Finally, Bella surfaced. "I . . . I don't understand . . ."

"It means," Indigo replied, "that they're going to buy our homes. That they're going to forcefully turn us out onto the streets so they can dig up the whole village. So they can look for . . . for . . . *bones* . . . or whatever the hell it is they're so interested in for 'national heritage' purposes."

Bella blinked several times. Then she straightened up in her chair. She looked to Robert, and then to Cassandra. For the longest time, Cassandra was certain she was going to ask her to explain, and Cassandra knew there would've been nothing for her to do — that she would've had no option but to release the floodgates . . . to tell them all she knew . . . and to explain why she hadn't said anything sooner.

"Well, that's it then," Bella replied. "We'll have to move out of Normonswold."

Indigo looked as though she had swallowed a pineapple. "We will do *no* such thing."

Bella examined her mother with a sober expression. "But, Mum, this is the *government* we're talking about. They won't just be doing this on a whim. They have the full backing of the country behind them. Endless administration and bureaucracy. They'll have five answers for every question we put to them."

Indigo bowed her head and glared. "Then let's get asking questions — we've fought off invaders before, we'll do it again. We'll show them what Normonswold is made of."

This statement was greeted with a long silence.

Cassandra looked up. She had the sense she was being watched. As she cast her gaze across the café, she caught sight of the Old Couple themselves.

Geoff and Dee.

They stood at the counter; the two of them well into their eighties now.

The way Bella spoke about Geoff and Dee, Cassandra found it difficult to believe there had ever been a time when they hadn't existed in Normonswold.

And yet it seemed as if that time was fast approaching.

It was Dee who spoke. "We've had a good run. I suppose we always expected something like this to happen. Perfect never lasts forever."

Cassandra breathed in deeply, wondering whether Dee was aware she was about to feel Indigo Miles's wrath for voicing her fatalism. However, when Cassandra looked to Indigo, she was caught off guard by her measured expression. It seemed as if Cassandra had come across perhaps the only person walking the planet who Indigo respected.

When Indigo finally spoke, her voice was frail and childlike, as if she would forever be a little girl in the Old Couple's eyes. "Is it really over this time?"

Dee looked at her, then at her husband Geoff. "I think it might be."

33

CHANGE OF PLAN

*F*inn found it almost impossible to stay still. He was constantly taking a step forward, or one back. And then, realising these movements failed to extinguish his nervous energy, he trod side to side, scuffing his heels in the dirt.

He looked up the road, expecting to see a dirty white van come barrelling around the corner at any given moment. The twins — well, Petunia — had decided that they could now afford a greater budget for the purposes of the 'documentary' he was producing. Their first demand had been that Finn provide multiple camera angles . . . that he create a 'more professional' effort. He had bitten his tongue when he had had the urge to theorise on exactly what professionalism even was — and that it certainly did not equate to lashings of cash.

If anything, the opposite applied.

For better or worse, though, he had agreed to Petunia's demands. There was a kind of grim longing which made him want to see this through to the end. He had got himself into the situation, and he was the only one who could get himself out.

He had decided he was going to do the very best work he was capable of.

So that there might be something positive to come out of this.

Even as he stood at the side of the road, though, he couldn't keep his mind from sweeping back to Cassandra. He thought and thought and thought about her. It didn't matter what he fixed his mind on — if he set his concentration on appraising a camera angle, or attempting to get the balance of light just right — Cassandra would come leaping out from his subconscious, strangling all hope of logical thought straight out of his skull.

He supposed it would take time for all this to go away.

For him to *forget* her.

After he had betrayed her so badly, he deserved nothing more than to be forgotten himself . . .

It was then he saw a vehicle rounding the corner. He fixed his attention onto it. Realised that it wasn't by any means a white van — that this vehicle hadn't the space to accommodate half a dozen people with their technical equipment.

It was, in fact, a hatchback.

And it took him only a couple more moments to realise who was behind the wheel.

Dorothy.

Finn had come to know Dorothy well during his time in Normonswold, although they had hardly spoken more than a few words to one another. It seemed as if the phrase 'his reputation precedes him' had been solely invented for him.

Finn fully expected Dorothy to drive on by. He expected that the best he could hope for — now that he had aligned himself with evil forces — was a half-hearted wave. And yet, as Dorothy closed in, he began to slow.

That was when more dramatic thoughts began to strike.

He wondered if Dorothy was going to lull him into a false sense of security and then run him over. Perhaps Cassandra had put him up to that.

It wasn't like Finn *really knew* Dorothy all that well . . . and he *was* all alone out here in the countryside. Nobody would have to know exactly *who* had run him over if Dorothy did a thorough job.

Right as Finn was preparing to dive into the ditch at the side of the road, Dorothy slowed up. It was only when Finn was convinced it was a physical impossibility for Dorothy to run him over that he allowed himself to relax.

Dorothy stopped the car and wound the driver's window down. Finn saw right away that Dorothy was dressed in a suit. He supposed he was coming home from work. "Hi," Dorothy said, somewhat anticlimactically.

"Hi."

"Are you, uh, looking for a ride into town?"

Finn parted his lips to respond. He looked up the road, expecting to see the van containing his reinforcements arriving now. But there was still no sign of them. "Actually," Finn started, "I'm waiting . . ." but his words trailed off before he could finish.

Dorothy picked up the slack. "Want to take a drive?"

Finn thought to reiterate what he had just said, but it seemed as if his resolve was completely broken. A slight smile snuck onto his lips. He looked around, half expecting to see either Petunia or Titania Knightly standing nearby, keeping watch, making sure he didn't escape before he had gone through with what he had promised.

Before he had gone through with what they were paying him to do.

There was no sign of them, though.

He turned back to Dorothy. "All right."

———

For the longest time, Finn just stared out of the window at the countryside blurring past. He thought Dorothy would make a beeline for Normonswold, but he instead took a roundabout route. It appeared that Dorothy was serious about them 'going for a drive'.

"What do you think about Cass?" Dorothy asked.

Finn was taken off-guard by the simple nature of the question. Or maybe it was just the unfussy nature with which he asked it. "I . . . think I love her."

"You *think* you love her?"

"Yes."

Dorothy drove on for several moments, hands gripping the steering wheel tightly. Finn couldn't help but notice that Dorothy had recently got a manicure, and that he had pearl-toned finger-nails. That his hands looked extremely well moisturised. "Can you remember what your life was like before you met her?"

Finn thought about this. He thought about all of the adventures he had been on. All of the wonderful projects he had had the plea-sure of participating in. And then he thought about all of the people he had met along the way. And then he thought about how he had never felt a connection like the one he shared with Cassandra.

The one they *had* shared.

Before he had ruined everything.

"It sounds stupid to say it, but I can't remember what my life was like before."

"Can you imagine your life without her — going forward?"

"No."

Dorothy pouted. "Well, then, why're you wasting time?"

Finn broke out in a broad grin — what felt like his first smile in days. "It's not that simple. There's other stuff in play."

"Like what? Money? Contracts?"

"Yeah, actually," Finn responded, surprised and somewhat taken aback at just how perceptive Dorothy was. Or perhaps it spoke volumes for the velocity at which gossip travelled in a small town such as Normonswold. Finn was certain that absolutely nothing stayed a secret for long in a place like this.

Dorothy drove on. They passed through a wood — trees springing up on either side of the road. Finn felt himself going giddy as he attempted to trace the sky between the tree trunks. His heart was beating strongly against his throat.

Once they got through the trees, he realised that Normonswold was right on the horizon, and that they were heading towards the village.

"I've never seen it from this angle," Finn said.

"Not many people do," Dorothy replied. "Almost everyone goes the most direct route when they want to go to the village. They don't think of going up a hill, taking the scenic way through the trees . . . even when they're on holiday." He glanced at Finn. "Isn't it funny that we're always in a rush, no matter what — work or recreation?"

Finn thought his life was some kind of testament to *not* being in a rush. He had actively fought back against almost all traditional expectations which society placed on him and his 'career' . . . if it could even be called that.

And yet, he couldn't help but admit there was a fragment of truth in what Dorothy was saying. He *did* feel as if he was in a rush. As if he was in a rush to pass from *project to project* — as if he was in a rush to move from *place to place*.

Why was that?

"We're all running away from something," Dorothy said, bringing them down the hill, and onto the plains which approached Normonswold.

Finn could just about make out the copse of trees on the edge of the village which shrouded Ebbendevor: the Miles' family home.

They went on the rest of the journey in silence.

It seemed inevitable when Dorothy brought the car to a halt outside Molinaar's Cottage. He turned to Finn with a smile and bid him good luck.

It was the strangest feeling. It seemed as if there was no other option but to march up that path to the front door.

For him to return to Cassandra.

34

A GREAT SURPRISE

*C*assandra was lightly dozing — drifting in a half-dream — when she realised someone was knocking at the door. She unfolded herself from where she lay on her bed, feeling a fuzzy warmth at her feet. When she looked, she saw Woss had taken up his place there. That he had seen the opportunity for a comfortable sleeping spot and had seized it with both paws. He was unmoved as she gently extracted the soles of her feet from his belly and trod her way across her bedroom floor and then down the staircase. Even as she stood ready to open the door, she had the sense that it was him . . . that he had come back.

She waited for the longest time.

Then drew the door open.

It was as if she was still dreaming — the way the sun glimmered through the cloud, setting him in the foreground in an unreal kind of pose. Perhaps it was because she had never expected to see him again. Maybe it was because she had believed that he would finish whatever arrangement he had had commenced with the Knightly twins before getting out of town forevermore. Getting out of her life forevermore.

But he was back.

Before she could say anything at all — before she could *think* about how they had parted — emotion overwhelmed her. She launched herself into his arms.

There was a wobbly moment where he successfully managed to balance their weight, but then the two of them toppled over, falling onto the lush grass of the front garden of Molinaar's Cottage. Cassandra couldn't help but let loose a girlish giggle.

Then she kissed him long and hard.

She only surfaced when she heard a car engine hum into life.

Pinning him to the grass, she glanced over the wall of the front garden, seeing Dorothy's smiling face framed in the driver's side window. She watched as he drove up the road and then out of sight — leaving the two of them alone.

She turned back to Finn, feeling something overtake her. The smile which clung to her lips lessened its grip on her cheeks. "You've decided to stop what you're doing? You've made a choice?"

His arm still flung about her midriff, Finn looked her in the eye, then said, "There's some details to be taken care of, but — in a word — *yes.*"

She tried to work out whether or not he was telling the truth. And then — deciding there was no reason in the world for him not to — she decided to believe him. "You're staying, then?"

"Well, if there's anywhere to stay after things have finished."

It was only then that reality struck her, that she realised just what the state of play actually was. That the Knightly twins had succeeded in convincing the government that Normonswold needed to be torn down.

"What did Dorothy say to you to make you come back?"

Finn met her gaze. "We went for a drive."

She cracked a grin. "He can be awfully convincing when he gets you alone, can't he?"

"I would say so."

They lay in the grass for what felt like an hour or more. Nobody passed them by on the street. She wondered if they were experiencing some sort of an enchanted moment. As if the world stood still for the two of them — allowing them some time to get their breath back. But — clearly — it couldn't last forever.

There was the *hum* of an approaching car, and Cassandra glanced up to see George behind the wheel. Harriet was in the passenger seat. When the car pulled up and they stepped out, she saw that Bella and George had been sitting in the back.

Cassandra felt a tremble pass through her stomach. It set a skitter passing up her spine to see their faces — to see how drawn their expressions were. She knew that Normonswold meant much more to all of them than a mere HQ for the company they had built together. This place had become their home.

And now it was to be destroyed.

There had to be *something* they could do.

When Bella cast her eyes over Finn and Cassandra hurriedly getting themselves up off the front lawn, she gave the slightest of smiles — perhaps glad for this brief, amusing diversion. "Well, I see you two have kissed and made up." Whatever trace of a smile had appeared disappeared now. She gave a sigh. "We managed to fumble together a meeting with Sylvia. She did all she could. No luck, though."

Cassandra thought of the year before, when they had met Kareema Ashburton. And then how — upon her death, not far from here, in the woods just outside Normonswold — her personal assistant-cum-personal physician had inherited her affairs.

It was something which Cassandra hadn't even thought about until this moment. And now she did, she felt as if all the air had been knocked out of her lungs. Of course they had needed to go to Sylvia for help. She *surely* possessed the connections to sort out the situation. To save Normonswold . . . except — from what Bella was saying — it appeared she did not.

Bella continued, "She said she was very sorry but that it wasn't in her philosophy — or that of Kareema — to influence or get involved with politics in any way. She wants nothing to do with the government. She said the conditions of the promise she made to Kareema were unambiguous."

When Cassandra thought of Kareema Ashburton's legacy and the government, she couldn't help but think of two ships passing in the night. A pair of goliaths sizing one another up, as if in a perpetual state of readiness for a fight which could easily destroy them both.

Cassandra looked to Finn, and then to the others. "What can we do, then?" she asked.

Bella looked to Robert, then George and Harriet. Finally, she turned her attention back to Cassandra. "I don't think there's anything left for us *to* do . . . when the legacy-protectors like my mother, or the Old Couple, decide that the time is right for us to give up the ghost and move on with our lives, then perhaps that's what we should do."

Cassandra thought back to the afternoon in Old Couple's café, still unable to quite believe she had witnessed what she had. There was such a sense of defeat about the whole thing. But who was she to declare Normonswold *must* be saved?

"Cup of tea?" Bella said, putting on a perky voice, and treading her way up the front path. "Or maybe you two would prefer a glass of lemonade — something to cool you down?"

The six of them had hardly taken their places at the table when the front door swung open without warning. They all turned to look. It was Frieda Smyth, proprietor of the Thicket Arms Inn.

As always, she wore a sour-mouthed expression, as if someone held a rotten carton of milk right beneath her nostrils. She glared about the kitchen as if they were the ones who were intruding upon her home, and not the other way around.

"What's all this I hear about town getting flattened?"

For a moment, nobody seemed to have the guts to answer.

Then Cassandra regained her balance.

"Uh, they're knocking it down for reasons of 'national heritage'."

" 'National heritage' ." Frieda spat the phrase as if it was a curse. "And Normonswold doesn't form a part of national heritage? Aren't we *important* enough to be included? Are we not *old* enough?"

Bella sighed. "That's about the long and the short of it."

Frieda pursed her lips. Then shook her head. With a short, sharp breath inward — followed by an abrupt exhale — she stared at them all once again. There was an unsettling element to her gaze which made whoever fell under it want nothing more than to wriggle away and escape as soon as possible. And Cassandra was no different.

"Well," Frieda continued, "what're *you* all going to do about it, then?"

"What're *we* going to do about it?" Bella asked. "Nothing — there's nothing to do."

"I don't believe you."

"I'm sorry?"

"I don't *believe* there's nothing you can do."

If it had been anybody else, Cassandra was sure Bella would have risen to the bait — that she would've been quick to give some sort of biting retort. She would've thrown the question right back.

But nobody threw anything at Frieda.

Not even words.

Apparently sensing she held her foot on their collective throat, Frieda continued, "Look around you. There are others who want to help. There are others who want to fight for their homes. They might not have put up their hands when you had that silly old protest against that lord and his leisure resort, but they'll stand with you now. They'll do all they can to help — I assure you of that. Their homes are at stake. Their *lives* are at stake."

As if Frieda had given too much away, she blinked several times, returning from a trancelike state. During her speech, the line of her mouth had softened slightly. Not into a smile, but into something which no longer resembled her trademark perpetual frown. Apparently noting this, Frieda squeezed her lips together again, nodded once, then turned on her heel and stomped out of Molinaar's Cottage — bringing the door shut with an almighty slam.

Cassandra looked about the table, to the bemused expressions, the undrunk cups of tea. She tried to think of some quip to lighten the mood, but nothing occurred to her.

Nothing occurred to any of them.

35

A MIDSUMMER SURPRISE

*C*assandra had come to dread the arrival of the post in the mornings. It was difficult to believe there had been a time when she had been excited. When each day, something great would arrive. A new order. Or a handwritten note from a fan — some touching story about how one of the cards had come to bear on some monumental personal event. She relished reading these letters with Bella. They often ended up having a good cry together. Now, though, the act of collecting the post was filled with nothing but dread — dread that there would be some fresh missive from the government, concerning the CPOs which'd been placed upon Normonswold.

The letter declaring the date on which they all had to *get out*.

Cassandra's hands trembled as she stooped to pick up the bundle of letters. She scanned them all immediately. She was glad to see there was no sign of anything formal, official-looking. As she brought the post to the kitchen table, she couldn't help but wonder if the letter would perhaps come in some friendly wrapping. If the government offices would somehow conspire to lull them into a false sense of security with a handwritten envelope — 'a charm offensive' as they called it — only to reveal the cold, hard fact within:

The deadline.

However, as Cassandra made her way through the envelopes, she found none contained anything of that order. When she reached the last envelope, she had to admit she was deeply anxious. She felt as if some cosmic force was setting her up to be knocked down in dramatic fashion. And yet, as she slit the envelope and withdrew the folded-over page from within, she still couldn't make herself believe this wasn't anything from the government. That it was — in fact — from Indigo Miles.

An invitation.

Three invitations, to be specific.

One for Bella. Another for Harriet. And one for Cassandra.

To begin with, she didn't quite absorb what the fancy writing on the invitations was saying. She was confused by the cursive lettering, telling herself time and again she was misinterpreting the text. But there could be no other explanation.

There it was in — albeit loopy and fancy — black and white:

Indigo Miles and Peter Hauntspath invite you to celebrate the event of their marriage on Saturday, 31st July, 20—, at five o'clock in the evening.

Cassandra didn't get much further than that before she heard footfall on the staircase. She glanced up to see Bella walking through the doorway, still dressed in her pyjamas and stifling a yawn with the back of her hand. As she approached the kitchen counter, and the kettle — clearly set on brewing her morning coffee — she murmured, "Anything good in the post?" over her shoulder.

Cassandra stood still, feeling as if she was some kind of crook caught with her hand in the till. "Uh, well . . ." and she handed over the invitation to Bella.

As she watched Bella's eyes flicker back and forth across the page, she expected fireworks. She was ready for anything. For Bella to crunch the invitation into a ball and toss it across the room — or for her to grab her by the throat in a classic kill-the-messenger move.

She was not prepared when Bella cracked a smile and shook her head.

"Mum could've at least used a Humble invitation." She shrugged then sighed. "Well, I suppose I'd better give her a ring to congratulate her. I imagine she is nervously awaiting my official approval."

And with that — with Cassandra feeling somewhat shell-shocked by the whole encounter — Bella slipped out of the room.

It went without saying that the time leading up to the wedding was manic. It seemed as if Indigo Miles turned up at Molinaar's Cottage every single day in a state of distress about something or other. Every time Cassandra heard a knock at the door — usually when she was in the middle of sketching some detail or other — she raised her head and watched on as Bella went to meet her mother; as she went to deal with the Disaster of the Day.

With all of the commotion over the wedding, it was almost excusable that everybody forgot about the compulsory purchase orders hanging over the entire village. It was only after a week or so of Bella's constant nurturing of her mother's wedding plans that Cassandra realised it would be down to her to effect some kind of a resistance. At least she had Finn on her side, and he was truly a worthy ally . . . especially given his insider's knowledge about the enemy.

In between sketching sessions, Cassandra and Finn would sit in the studio and think through the situation, trying to work out what the way forward might be. They covered all of the usual well-worked bases for situations such as these. All of the various protests which might be employed:

Physical manifestations, written petitions . . . undercover sabotage.

When Lord Charles had strolled into town with ideas about constructing his leisure complex, the village had used a little of everything. Now, though, no matter how hard Cassandra and Finn thought on the issue, there seemed to be nothing which would make a definite difference — swing the tide in their favour.

At the end of such a brainstorming meeting, Finn became exasperated, throwing up his hands and falling back onto the sofa. Cassandra had to admit she felt like doing the same. They were responsible for an impossible undertaking.

But then she thought about what Frieda Smyth had said.

That they could depend on the villagers' help.

With Finn somewhat reluctantly trailing on her heels — goodness knew, having lived at the Thicket Arms these past weeks and months he had had enough of Frieda Smyth to last a lifetime — they went to pay her a visit.

As always, Frieda Smyth gave the impression she was irrecoverably busy. She was dedicating herself to polishing the brass railings on the front desk. Expecting Frieda either to ignore them or deny she had ever made any such statement, she was rendered surprised when Frieda straightened up, laid her polishing rag down on the front desk, and gestured for them to follow her into the back room.

Cassandra had to admit she had never spent much time in imagining the exact condition of the room behind the front desk at the Thicket Arms Inn, but now she was experiencing it for the first time, she wondered if she hadn't had in mind a dishevelled, pokey little hole. She had had the vague idea that it would be dark; cardboard boxes stacked up; dust filling the air. However, nothing could've been further from the truth.

The back room was light, and it was tidy, and the air was decidedly fresh . . . this was owing to the window thrown open onto the garden.

There was a bookcase pushed up against one of the walls, and Frieda made a beeline for it. She pulled free an old tome. As she laid it down upon the desk, Cassandra noted the book was untouched by dust.

Cassandra and Finn stood over Frieda as she turned the pages.

Within were various hand-drawn maps. She decided the squiggly line represented the river, and that the scribbled trees were the woods. Then there were the disordered, mismatching squares which couldn't be anything but houses. Perhaps if she had been born into another era Cassandra would've been a cartographer — there was something about the practice which looked like a lot of fun . . . and there had been a certain degree of artistic licence before the innovation of satellite navigation which had reduced — or elevated, depending on your perspective — so many things to a science.

One of the mismatched squares caught Cassandra's eye. She read the cursive lettering and found herself saying the words out loud. "The Thicket Arms Inn."

Frieda broke into a grin — the first time that Cassandra had ever seen her show off her teeth in anything other than a snarl. "My ancestors," she said, proudly.

Cassandra exchanged glances with Finn, afraid to venture anything further.

Frieda kept turning the pages, eventually settling on one in particular. She looked up at Cassandra and Finn with something approximating a smile. "Do you see?"

To begin with, Cassandra thought Frieda might be attempting to strike some cloying tone — that she was trying to get them to suggest something so she could bat it down with glee. However, Cassandra realised she was genuinely interested in what they thought. So she set her mind to the task.

"I . . . can't say I do," Cassandra replied, shifting Finn a sidelong glance.

"This map shows the village of Normonswold as is covered by the founding documents." Frieda traced a line with her finger. "Look. This was the boundary."

Cassandra did her best to render this crude map in her mind — to square it with her perception of the reality as it was today. But even with her imagination, she found it a trying task. In the end, she gave up. "Where would that be in modern times?"

"At the end of the high street — before it turns off onto the country road."

Cassandra understood now.

Frieda turned the page, revealing another map of the local area, then continued, "This shows the original Knightly Estate, as it was first granted."

Cassandra saw how there were several fields between the Knightly Estate and Normonswold. A respectable buffer zone . . . although perhaps too close for comfort when it came to the Knightlies.

"Up on the shelf" — Frieda nodded to the bookcase — "there's a whole host of volumes which document the gradual creep of the Knightly Estate, closer and closer to the village, as they bought up land, as they took firmer control. This was what led to the expansion of Normonswold — the influx of workers."

Finn spoke up for the first time. "And did the Knightlies expand their influence by wholly honourable means?"

Frieda gave him a devilish smile. "The fact you're asking that question makes me think you already know the answer."

They'd spent the best part of two hours with Frieda when Cassandra realised that although it was wonderful to have made a few cracks in Frieda's formidable armour, it was time for them to get down to business. She examined Frieda, replacing the current tome on the shelf, and said, "This is all fascinating but how do you expect this to change the government's mind?"

"You've seen for yourselves, the Knightlies have waged a centuries' old campaign against Normonswold. From these volumes, it's *clear* that they have wanted to get shot of the village. They have made numerous attempts to absorb the place into their estate, and this is merely the latest."

Finn broke in. "But aren't you missing something important in that argument?"

A dark colour passed over Frieda's face and Cassandra couldn't help thinking that something of the Frieda everybody knew and rightly feared had re-emerged.

Clearly not wanting to enrage her any further, Finn continued, "I mean, it's not that they're *extending* their estate — they told me they will be tearing the whole place down. Everything Lord Charles built for his leisure complex. They don't seem to care about the land any longer. They just want to get shot of the whole lot."

Frieda stared back into Finn's eyes. Almost a pitying expression. "I'm sure the sisters told you how their estate was burned to the ground. And that it was the villagers who were to blame? That their fancy manor house is buried under all that muck?"

"Yes."

"Well, anybody who knows anything about *anything* knows that's a complete lie. The villagers had nothing to do with it. *Everybody* knows the Knightlies have always been the most appalling drunks. There were witnesses that night at the estate, too. It was a party — another lavish one which the master of the house was in a habit of throwing . . . a fire got started; I imagine from a discarded cigar or a neglected fire."

Cassandra thought about this. She took hold of Finn's hand. There was something about being in Frieda's company which made her feel greatly uneasy, even when she was being cooperative . . . even when she was helping achieve a common goal.

Finn, though, managed to maintain his courage. "So what would be the plan? That we would approach the government — tell them the discovery of the passageway was all some ruse so the Knightlies might have their revenge on Normonswold? A kind of malicious swansong?"

Frieda locked Finn in her glare. It was one of those pauses where Cassandra thought she might have to rush Finn from the room before Frieda scratched his eyes out. However, when Frieda did speak, it was in a level, clear-headed tone.

"There's one more book I have to show," she said. "But I don't know if I can trust the two of you — being outsiders, and all."

Cassandra's instinct was to protest — to shoot back that she *lived* in Molinaar's Cottage. That she wasn't an 'outsider'. But she realised that in Frieda's eyes she would always be an outsider. Frieda would not be content until many generations from now when Cassandra's descendants had bled into the Normonswold soil.

Cassandra hardened her resolve. "I suppose it comes down to whether or not you trust we truly want to save Normonswold. Whatever you have to show us, it seems you need our help — a pair of *outsiders* — otherwise you would've taken the information you have and used it to save Normonswold yourself."

Frieda fixed her with a cold stare, and Cassandra immediately regretted having spoken at all. Now she was the one feeling the chill of fear creeping through her blood.

Frieda, however, did not argue. "Very well," she replied, turning back to the bookshelf. She spent a good minute or so searching — long enough that Cassandra thought she might've misplaced the volume or, worse, that it might've been stolen.

In the end, though, she located the tome. She laid it upon the desk.

There was no need for anybody to say anything.

Frieda peeled back the cover.

Cassandra saw the village again. Thick black lines snaked outside the village boundaries. She looked up, meeting Finn's eyes, and then Frieda's.

"The Piracy Passage," she said.

WHITE WEDDING

*A*s expected, on the morning of Indigo Miles and Peter Hauntspath's wedding everything was manic. Cassandra did her best to maintain her calm, ducking and diving out of Bella's way as she went through a multitude of outfits in her search for the One Perfect Look. Cassandra sorted out her own outfit in a matter of minutes — pawing through the wardrobe and pulling out a pale pink dress which she thought suited the occasion without upstaging the bride. But, then again, she had never really been in the business of upstaging anybody . . .

As she left the bathroom, she overheard Robert asking Bella whether she was nearly ready. Judging from Bella's cutting response, Cassandra decided to skip out of Molinaar's Cottage before a full-blown fight erupted.

She barely made it two steps down the front path before almost knocking the postwoman flat on her back. The two of them took stock of one another, both as surprised by the sudden encounter. When she looked down, she saw the postwoman was holding out a handful of letters. Her pulse racing, she took them, muttering some word of thanks. Over her shoulder, Bella shouted something.

Cassandra didn't pause to ask her to repeat it.

As she made her way down the street, she felt strangely naked not to have a man on her arm. There was something about wearing a dress like this — and going to a wedding — which brought out something achingly traditional.

This issue was soon resolved when she stopped by the Thicket Arms Inn, where Finn was waiting in the reception area. He wore a simple suit with a maroon tie, and Cassandra was surprised at just how handsome he looked in a formal outfit.

It sent her heart racing.

"Well," he said. "You look lovely." And he kissed her on the lips.

A tingling sensation took hold of her gut.

He pulled away, fixing his gaze on the letters she held. "What've you got there?"

She couldn't help but smile broadly as she held the bundle out. "Morning post."

"You brought it with you?"

She thought about the scene as she had left Molinaar's Cottage behind. "There wasn't really any other option."

"Anything good?"

Cassandra looked at the letters again — only really seeing them for the first time. There were several bills, as was standard. She slipped them to the bottom of the pile. This left her with a single letter, which looked ominous.

"You think this is it?" Finn asked.

She drew a deep breath. She thought about how they had taken multiple scans of the books Frieda Smyth had shown them. And how they had searched for the right governmental department to send everything to — and then how they had spent hours writing the letter in such a way that it *had* to convince them that Normonswold was being made a victim of the Knightly family.

Now, though, as she held the letter — what might be the answer they had longed for — she couldn't help but feel that it had all been in vain.

That it had all *obviously* been in vain.

Hands trembling, she tore open the envelope, feeling Finn's eyes on her fingers as she did so. When she removed the letter within, she nearly allowed it to slip from her hands and flutter down to the ground. But she managed to hold on.

"What does it say?" Finn asked.

She pressed her lips firmly together and set about reading.

Within seconds, she had her answer.

There was no need for her to read the formal niceties.

"No," she said, looking up. "They say *no*."

Finn remained very still. She could feel his warm breath against her neck. There was something about having him near which reassured her, which prevented her from completely breaking down. She was certain she would've done so if she had been alone. They had put so much effort into saving the village. And everything had been relying upon this one letter. At the bottom of everything, she had been so sure they would win in the end. But she had been naïve.

It seemed the story of her life.

When he asked to see it, she handed the letter over.

Even as she felt numb and empty inside, there was a hope which continued to warm her — a sense that Finn might be able to read something between the lines which she had overlooked.

But he had nothing.

"Okay," he said, "I suppose we'll have to enjoy the time we have left." He glanced up. "I guess we'll have to make this wedding a celebration for all sorts of reasons."

"I'm not telling anybody about this — not until the festivities are over."

"Agreed."

The two of them had almost made their way out of the Thicket Arms Inn when a familiar voice stopped them in their tracks.

"You did your best."

They turned.

Frieda Smyth stood behind the reception desk — having emerged from the back room. She was wearing an icy-blue trouser suit with a frilly, floppy hat. "I want to thank you for trying."

Despite the sombre tone, Cassandra couldn't help but blurt out what was on her mind. "You're coming to the wedding?"

Frieda looked to Finn and then Cassandra. She seemed a little startled, as if she had surprised even herself by accepting Indigo Miles's wedding invitation. "It'd be a waste to have got dressed up for nothing, wouldn't it?"

Ebbendevor had never looked as gorgeous as it did on the day of Indigo Miles's wedding, although Cassandra was unsure how she had expected anything else. Indigo Miles made everything spectacular — no matter the occasion . . .

White bunting streamed from the tree branches. There was white silk all over the place, draped across tables, over the backs of chairs. Ebbendevor itself hung with white banners. Then there were the flowers.

Each table had its own centrepiece, and then there were the

white rose petals which had been scattered across the ground to mark the trail to the altar.

Finn, Cassandra and Frieda followed the path.

The altar had been constructed around the back of the house, beside the creek which ran by the bottom of the lawn. This too was white, and had been strung with all sorts of flowers. Already, several guests had arrived. There couldn't be more than ten, fifteen minutes before the ceremony was due to start.

Waiting staff dressed in waistcoats — and white gloves, as Cassandra observed — bobbed between groups of people, offering them flutes of champagne and hors d'oeuvres.

Cassandra felt uncomfortable, almost as if she was under-dressed. She was glad to feel Finn's reassuring touch at the small of her back. His fingertips sent warm waves flowing through her blood.

She glanced about for any sign of Bella and Robert, but she couldn't see either. She wondered if they had managed to navigate the tricky matter of Bella's dress without further issue . . .

She shifted her attention back onto her surroundings.

Onto the day ahead.

She knew — no matter what Finn had said, about them enjoying the moment as best they could, in the knowledge that Normonswold was doomed — she wouldn't be able to shake the letter from her mind. It would continue to lurk in the background.

Never forgotten.

She wondered if she shouldn't make some sort of public service announcement — letting everybody know the truth that the appeal had failed . . . that the faith which they had placed in her and Finn had not been repaid.

All of a sudden, she felt as if she was sinking.

A deeply uncomfortable sensation.

It was only when Finn spoke to her, indicating they should move in the direction of the altar, in preparation for the couple's arrival, that she stirred from the pit she had envisioned springing up on all sides.

They took their seats with the other guests. Frieda sat beside them, despite having the option of sitting beside any other villager. The letter had at least achieved something. She and Finn appeared to have won Frieda's respect.

It was only when the organist began to play that Cassandra even noticed there were musicians. She looked over to the side of the altar, realising that a pair of violinists accompanied the organist. They began to play a joyful tune — not the wedding march; not yet. And then she noticed the registrar; dressed in her suit and tie, holding a leather-bound wallet down at her waist. Everything was in place. Everything was ready.

Just a few more details to go.

At that moment, Cassandra looked around and noticed Bella and Robert trotting towards them, taking their places among the crowd. As they sat down, Cassandra caught Harriet's eye, and exchanged a smile, while George remained sombre, staring wistfully at the altar.

Cassandra felt her stomach clench. She looked about the audience, wondering if anybody else felt nervous for Indigo and Peter. Or did they truly believe that the two of them were incapable of feeling such emotions? That the two of them were such well-assured, self-confident individuals that to feel such a way would have been ridiculous?

The musicians fell silent and then began to play the wedding march.

As one, the audience rose, looking towards Ebbendevor, to the back of the house. It was through the lofty white pillars that Indigo and Peter emerged. The two of them walking arm-in-arm as they had clearly prearranged.

Cassandra observed their advance across the back lawn, taking stock of Indigo's wedding dress. It came to a halt just below the knee while — up top — showing off plenty of her elegant, ivory shoulders.

If Cassandra had been at all sceptical about the wedding previously, then now she had no reason to doubt. She had no choice but to acknowledge the way Indigo and Peter looked at one another. The two of them entirely taken. As she glanced about the crowd, she caught sight of Adiema — Harriet's aunt — and noticed how she was staring at Indigo and Peter with great longing. Or maybe that was just Cassandra's imagining.

The registrar led Indigo and Peter through the service. She might as well have been a tape recording because the two of them hardly seemed to notice her presence — unable to tear their eyes away from each other.

Cassandra squeezed Finn's hand. A short burst of warmth ploughed through her.

As the registrar led Indigo and Peter through the final stages of the ceremony, Dorothy rose up from the front row. Today he wore a floaty, pink number. From within a box, he held out the rings to Indigo and Peter. This done, Dorothy took up his seat again, though not without a beaming grin to the assembled audience.

When the registrar closed her book and pronounced Indigo and Peter married, someone in the audience let out a cry of delight.

Apparently swept up in the rush of emotion, Peter rocked Indigo back in his arms and planted a kiss upon her lips.

When Cassandra sneaked a glanced over the audience, she couldn't help her attention falling upon Bella and Robert; to see the way Robert was squirming in his seat. She looked over to Harriet and George, seeing that he too was in a similar state.

Weddings, she reflected, were a wonderful way of seeing into a man's mind . . . of seeing what the immediate future might hold.

She didn't dare look at Finn.

CELEBRATED UNION

*O*nce the ceremony was over and done with, the musicians traded their violins and organ in for brass instruments and a keyboard, meanwhile a drummer and a singer joined their ensemble. Before Cassandra had really had the time to digest the ceremony itself, it seemed as if the spectacle before her eyes had utterly transformed — as was so often the way with Indigo Miles's famed parties. They were living, breathing things . . . photographs could never do them justice — just blurry, impressionist images.

Dinner was served from a buffet, and the guests set about the food provided with great gusto — Cassandra and Finn not excused by any means. Once they had all filled their bellies, the festivities truly took hold.

Despite the general sense of glee and delight surrounding her, Cassandra couldn't help but feel a certain weight at the back of her mind. She thought about the demolition of Normonswold, Ebbendevor would be gone too.

Looking about the garden party, she could see everyone was having a wonderful time. Champagne was flowing. People danced together.

Maybe this was a kind of funeral, too . . .

Still, it appeared Finn was just as reluctant to let go completely as she was — with all of the worries of what was to come clearly weighing upon his mind, too. They moved together to the orchestra, struggling to keep up with the frenetic pace of the band and the other dancers. After a few numbers, she led them off to one of the chairs at the side of the dance floor. The two of them sat and watched. As she examined Finn's face in profile, she saw he wasn't smiling.

"We did our best," Cassandra said. "But there was nothing to be done."

Finn pressed his lips tightly together. "It still doesn't feel enough — it feels as if we could've done more . . . if we'd just said things differently in the letter. If we'd, maybe, spent more time going through Frieda's bookshelf . . . perhaps there would've been something else which might've leaped out at us . . . something which would've swung the case."

"But there wasn't . . . and there *isn't* anything we can do, okay?"

Indigo was approaching the band. She looked gorgeous in her wedding dress — there was something about Bella in her face, but also something else . . . something which marked her out as being a force of nature.

Just exactly what it was, Cassandra never could quite put her finger on.

Indigo Miles never stood still long enough.

The wedding had already eschewed convention in so many ways it hardly mattered that speeches were taking place, following dinner, in the midst of dancing. Or that it would be the bride herself — rather than the father of the bride, or the bridegroom, or the best man — who was set to make the speech.

Peter stood at the side of the stage.

The band reached a crescendo and then gradually wound down — the drummer ending the current number with a couple of cymbal crashes.

The dancers stepped apart, and everyone's eyes focused upon the stage.

Indigo took the microphone — beaming. "Friends — dear *friends!*"

The guests roared back in response. Fervour more akin to a sporting occasion. Cassandra supposed this was only testament to Indigo's popularity.

"It has been a *pleasure* of the deepest and most wonderful kind to have you all here today on this *wonderfully* happy occasion. On behalf of myself and my husband — Peter Hauntspath — I would like to thank you all *dearly* for attending today's ceremony." She looked out across the crowd, drawing a deep breath.

Cassandra glanced to Peter, still standing at the side of the stage. She couldn't help but think that Peter was somewhat trapped — unsure whether he should get up and join his wife, or if he should remain in the shadows a while longer lest he upstage her . . .

When Indigo spoke again, Cassandra was surprised to hear the slight break in her voice — the emotion of the situation clearly getting to her. Cassandra couldn't help but feel somewhat ashamed for having believed Indigo incapable of such vulnerability. She supposed it had to do with her extroverted nature — how it seemed she could bat away any sort of sentiment with nothing more than a wiggle of her little finger.

"Peter and I met under random circumstance. When I first laid eyes upon him, I thought that he must be some sort of a travelling salesperson . . ."

The crowd chuckled.

". . . However, I soon grew to understand he was a film director. That he was an *artist.*" She looked across the crowd. "Just like my daughter, Bella. And if there is something for which artists can never be accused of then it is a lack of passion. Peter decided to stay here — in Normonswold — on the whim that he might have the hope of *wooing* me."

Someone gave a wolf whistle.

Even from where Cassandra was standing, she could've sworn Indigo flushed slightly. As soon as she noticed this detail, though, the normal colour returned to her face. She regained her footing.

"Well, in that I can reveal — *dear audience* — that he was successful."

A round of spontaneous applause rippled through the crowd.

Another wolf whistle.

Cassandra couldn't help but grin broadly. She felt Finn give her hand a squeeze.

Indigo seemed lost for words. This momentary lapse did not last long, however. "Never was a fan of drawn-out speeches. Always thought they were the *most* self-indulgent thing." She snapped her fingers at the nearby waiter, who, responding to this command, brought her a flute of champagne on a silver tray.

Cassandra noticed how there was waiting staff all among the crowd now, and that they were giving out champagne to everybody. She and Finn took theirs.

Once Indigo was content everybody had a drink in their hand, she continued. "I toast the future; my and Peter's union, and all of the future unions which take place in this village, and beyond." She broke into a devilish grin. "Go forth and *multiply!*"

With that she held up her champagne for a good few seconds — like an actress on stage holding up a dagger before plunging it with great finality into her breast.

She drank her glass down in one and then leaped from the stage, taking the dumbstruck Peter unawares. He just about managed to catch her in his arms, taking several unsure steps as he regained his balance.

With that, the dancing continued.

Perhaps it was the effect of the champagne, but Cassandra and Finn found themselves joining the festivities with greater gusto and abandon than before.

It was around midnight when the wedding party began to simmer down — when guests started to dribble away.

Cassandra remained fixed on the happy couple, watching as they twirled away, dancing with tireless enthusiasm. It was difficult for her to think of a time when she had ever seen a couple look so delighted by one another's company. To be quite honest, she had never seen a man who was content — or even vaguely *willing* — to dance for such a long time.

It must be love.

Speaking for herself, she couldn't say she was feeling all that enthusiastic about greeting the dawn in the back garden of Ebbendevor. With this on her mind, she drew Finn away from the dancing couples, away from the music, and towards a more secluded area. She dropped her voice to a whisper. "We need to tell them. They need to know the truth."

"But not on their wedding night," Finn replied. "We can keep it quiet till tomorrow, can't we?"

She looked back across the garden. Of course, she understood the logic of what Finn was saying, and yet she had always had some sort of a childlike, naïve sense that whenever she stumbled across the truth, she should take great pains to communicate it to those who were most likely affected by it. She couldn't help but feel it was a great deception for her to allow Indigo and Peter to dance away in the belief their future was secure — that she and Finn had launched what was sure to be a successful appeal against the plan to demolish the village — when nothing could've been further from the truth. And all this after Indigo had accepted her and Finn as part of their wedding.

As members of her inner circle.

It felt like a deep betrayal.

And yet . . . was there anything she could do?

Something made up her mind right then and there. Perhaps it was when her and Indigo's gaze crossed. Maybe something passed between the two of them telepathically. Whatever the explanation, Cassandra found herself pacing towards Indigo and Peter.

Although there were several other guests surrounding Indigo and Peter as they danced, their attention soon fell upon Cassandra. She supposed it must be the expression on her face. The rampant determination in her eyes.

"Can I have a word?!" Cassandra shouted to Indigo, over the band.

Indigo, with a broad grin, opened her eyes wide in faux delight and held out her arm so Cassandra might lead her away. Cassandra was glad Indigo had granted her a private audience so readily. Indigo would've been well within her rights to turn

Cassandra down . . . who was she to make demands of a bride on her wedding night?

The two of them stole away from the main guests and in through one of the back doors of the house. Although Cassandra expected Indigo to lead her just inside the doorway — so she might get through with what she had to say swiftly so she might return to the dancefloor — Indigo led her off into the Piano Room.

Cassandra had visited this particular room on several occasions. There was a grand piano which occupied much of the room, several framed photographs — a painting or two — of concert pianists in full flow. There was also a wide variety of furniture. And everything was impossibly comfortable.

Homely.

Indigo led her over to one of the sofas and they sat. Indigo reached out and clasped her hands. She looked her in the eye. "You're not pregnant, are you, dear?"

Cassandra almost burst into hysterical laughter. "There's something I need to tell you — something *else* I need to tell you."

"Okay," Indigo replied, leaning in close, her smile losing a little of its sharpness.

"It's about Normonswold . . . the future of the village . . . it's . . ."

Cassandra was distracted by the figure standing in the doorway. It took her several seconds to completely absorb who the figure actually was.

Dorothy.

As he had been earlier, when he had given the rings to the bride and groom, he was wearing a dress. His cheeks were flushed from all the dancing he had done that evening. The only thing about him which betrayed his otherwise jovial outward appearance was the absence of a smile on his lips. In fact, he looked grave-faced — his complexion ashen.

"I say, Dottie, dear," Indigo said, getting to her feet. "Are you feeling quite all right?"

Dorothy held himself still, meeting her eyes. Then he managed to summon a smile. "I . . . saw the two of you coming in here . . . wanted to see what all of the fuss was about."

"Ah," Indigo replied, shifting a glance at her. "Actually, I believe Cassandra wanted a private chat about something — a confidential conversation."

Dorothy looked from Indigo to Cassandra, then back again. "It won't take long — I promise. And if what I have to say doesn't interfere with what Cassandra has to tell you then I will leave you to it."

Indigo tilted her head to one side and spoke with a touch of impatience in her voice. "Well?"

Dorothy waited another moment before dishing out what he had to say. "I have spoken with the Knightly sisters, and they have agreed to do whatever they can to prevent the destruction of Normonswold. They have acknowledged the historical records Cassandra and Finnegan recovered from the Thicket Arms Inn. They will do their part in convincing the government that Normonswold need not be dug up — that people not be turfed out of their homes."

Cassandra felt as if she might explode. Somehow she found the words. "But, *how?*"

Dorothy remained still. The slightest of smiles appeared on his lips. "I just talked to them. I made them listen. They understood. It took time, but in the end they understood."

After a brief silence, Indigo said, "That's . . . wonderful news! *Brilliant!*" She looked to Cassandra. "Isn't that terrific?"

Cassandra held very still. She had begun to tremble. Something within her refused to believe what Dorothy had said. When she spoke, it was in monotone. Her lips moved despite the frozen expression on her face. "We got the news today — from the appeal — they turned us down . . . said that there was no alternative." She looked to Dorothy. "Maybe the twins have changed their mind about destroying Normonswold but what assurance do you have that the government will give so much as an inch on their already-declared plans?"

Dorothy eyed her. "I think you're underestimating just how much influence the Knightly sisters hold over decisions such as these . . . believe you me, they were most certainly privy to that appeal. Indeed, they were the ones who personally vetoed it."

"And you know this because they told you?"

Dorothy nodded. "I never had a chance to see the letter. When I turned up there, earlier today, I believed there was still time. That no decision had yet been made over the appeal. But they soon put me right. And then they allowed me to push them for the reasons they were pursuing the destruction of Normonswold, and I . . . well, I told them that they shouldn't do so any longer."

"But, *how*, dear?" Indigo said, eyeing Cassandra. "*How* did you convince them?"

"I just . . . opened up about myself . . . about my life . . . I used whatever I could to convince them. And they listened. They saw reason in the end."

Silence hung over them.

Suddenly, Indigo Miles clapped her hands together. "This *really* has been the most wonderful wedding a maiden could ever ask for! Really, truly, as if it wasn't enough that I have gained a husband, I have had my home, and my village, assured. I truly owe the two of you a great deal. You will be conscious enough to let me know if there is anything I can do for either of the two of you, won't you?"

Cassandra and Dorothy exchanged glances.

Indigo cracked a wide smile. "Good — *excellent!*" She jigged out of the Piano Room.

Cassandra and Dorothy stood there. The two of them with nothing to say to one another. Finally, Cassandra breached the silence. "Shall we re-join the party?"

EPILOGUE

*a*s Cassandra took in Molinaar's Cottage ahead — set in the glimmering, golden sunlight — she could barely believe she was coming home. That this was *truly* the place she lived. Where she worked.

When she looked to her side and saw Finn, she reached out and took hold of his hand. As always, his touch was reassuringly warm. It sent a pleasant tingle through her — breathing heat into her blood and bones.

Cassandra held her sketchpad down at her side while Finn had his camera slung over his shoulder. As had become their routine, they had gone down to the woods at first light. While Finn had set himself to filming backgrounds which would be used later on for a new range of virtual-reality greetings cards which Cassandra and Bella had developed, Cassandra had been etching whatever happened across her line of sight; looking for anything which might later spark her imagination.

Robert had thought long and hard before finding a place at

Humble Greetings for Finn, but he had been happy enough to offer him a contract — so he was a fully-fledged employee like the rest of them. When he had signed on the dotted line, Finn had joked it was the first real job he had ever had.

Cassandra had worried at first it might be too much too soon for Finn — that the commitment might serve only to scare him off ... but if his enthusiasm for the work he had done thus far was any kind of a measurement then he clearly had no regrets about the decision. In fact, although Cassandra would've felt uneasy saying it out loud, she had the feeling he had never been this content about his work.

The narrower, more-contained frame of Humble Greetings seemed to have acted as a focus point for his talent. It gave him something to aim for — something which he had to some degree lacked in the past.

The two of them smiling broadly, they trod on in through the front door, finding Bella, Robert, Harriet and George gathered around the kitchen table; the four of them with a cup of tea.

Some things were utterly consistent about Molinaar's Cottage — about Humble Greetings.

Cassandra and Finn joined the other four right away, being given their own cups of tea. That done, the six of them sat and talked about nothing much at all.

There was a lot of joking and laughter, though.

It was only when a knock came at the door that Cassandra felt a dose of reality strike. She had allowed herself to be swept away on the wave of good feeling which was brought on by companion-ship. Although she enjoyed nothing more than being alone and drawing in private, she still took a certain joy from being around others.

She had no idea what she expected upon opening the door —

perhaps to find herself face to face with a group of suited government officials, telling them they had all been duped, that their appeal had been rejected, after all.

That they had until midnight to get out . . . to get out of Normonswold.

However, when she opened the door, she found herself staring at Dorothy.

Today, he was wearing a white blouse over a pair of tight-fitting jeans. He wore a sunhat flopped at an angle. He stood with one hand perched at his waist. In the background, she could see his car parked up. She couldn't help noticing it was stuffed full of suitcases and boxes. "I've come to say goodbye."

Cassandra snapped back to Dorothy. "What?"

He just smiled and looked beyond her, into the cottage. "Is everyone here?"

"Yes."

"Do you think I could come in for a moment?"

"Of course."

She stood to one side, allowing Dorothy to pass into the front hall. She watched on as he trod his way to the kitchen. Everybody continued to make merry oblivious. When Dorothy reached the kitchen — Cassandra not far from his heels — everybody turned their attention to him. All of them grinning wildly.

Bella offered Dorothy a cup of tea, but he declined.

"I'm in a hurry," he replied. "You might say I have a plane to catch."

"A plane going where?"

Dorothy attempted a feeble smile. "It's a secret." He began to fidget with the buttons on his blouse.

Cassandra felt her gut clench tightly. She observed how the

smiles slipped from the mouths of those collected around the table.

Even Woss — who had been slumbering away in the corner — perked up, paying attention. Apparently channelling into the sudden blackening of the atmosphere.

"I . . . wanted to ask you about the cabin," Dorothy said. "I wanted to ask if you would like to take over . . . uh, I don't know what you'd call it . . . just look after it — that's all."

"Aren't you coming back?" Harriet asked.

The silence in the kitchen pressed hard against Cassandra's eardrums.

When Dorothy replied, his voice was broken — his tone cracked. "No. I'm not."

"Why?" Bella said.

"I . . . I've made my mind up not to return."

Cassandra told herself she needed to remain strong. Her voice somehow held firm. "We'll look after the cabin — of course we will."

Dorothy turned his attention onto her. He gave her a slight smile. "Thank you."

His eyes were damp.

Tears on the brink of spilling over.

"We should be thanking you," Bella said, getting to her feet. "Without you there wouldn't be any Normonswold. Without you, there would be no Humble Greetings."

Dorothy took a step back, to the front door.

Harriet got up. "Without Humble Greetings I have no idea where I would've gone."

"I never would've fulfilled my true potential," Cassandra put in.

Dorothy looked between the three girls, unable to decide which he should reply to. In the end, he said nothing — somewhere between shellshock and desperation.

It was Bella who took the initiative, throwing herself forward and embracing him. Then Harriet jumped in. Finally, after a moment's hesitation, Cassandra joined the group hug. The hug itself couldn't have lasted more than a minute — if that — but to Cassandra it encompassed so many things.

Relief.

Joy.

Hope.

Cassandra felt Dorothy had a clear sense of direction about where he was headed. At least he was sure. She had to respect his decision.

When they all broke apart, and Dorothy headed for the front door once again, it occurred to Cassandra to ask the question which was surely on all their minds. "Have you told Indigo yet?"

Dorothy hung back, a slight smile crossing his lips. "I thought I better leave her till last . . . I didn't want the whole village to know before I had told them myself."

Bella was measured. "She'll be devastated, you know. You will come back to visit, won't you?"

Dorothy pressed his lips tightly together then gave a gesture which might've been a nod, or a shake of the head. He ventured out of the front door.

Before he could get away, a thought struck Cassandra. "Wait!" she said, calling out. "Just a second!"

She dashed through the house to the studio, where she flipped through various folders, thumbing her way through the dozens and dozens — *hundreds?* — of sketches she had committed to paper. Finally, she reached the one she was searching for.

The one which featured Dorothy and Nameeth, walking away through the woods, leaving the cabin behind.

She slipped it into an envelope and returned.

Dorothy was already halfway down the garden path.

Cassandra jigged up to him, near enough thrusting the sketch into his chest.

He took it from her, beleaguered, but compliant.

She rose onto her tiptoes and whispered in his ear, "Don't open it until you're alone — until you need something to make you smile."

Dorothy gave her a strange expression, but thanked her all the same. Then he turned away, stepped through the open garden gate, got into his car and drove away.

Gone.

Perhaps forever.

———

That afternoon, Cassandra returned to the woods with Finn. Although they had got into the habit of staying about the house reading, watching films, or talking, it seemed appropriate given all that had happened that they return to the woods.

To the cabin.

The place which had been entrusted to their care.

Cassandra examined the logs which'd been carefully varnished — the elements which had been held at bay for so many years. All of the panes of glass which were perfectly intact . . . which had been kept so clean.

She felt Finn's warming breath on the back of her neck.

She turned.

And lost herself in his eyes.

He wrapped his arms around her.

As their mouths drew closer and closer together, she found herself uttering the words, almost beneath her breath. "Now we have somewhere — now we *all* have somewhere. Somewhere just for us."

THE END

AUTHOR'S NOTE

Thank you for taking the time to read one of my books. If you would like to hear about my latest releases you can sign up for my newsletter here: www.essiepowers.com

Thanks for reading!

Essie Powers

Humble Partings
The Third Humble Greetings Novel